KNOCKOUT GIRL

Natasja Eby

DEDICATION

For Josh "dedicate-your-next-book-to-me" Terry.
Thank you for being a friend.

ACKNOWLEDGMENTS

Thank you to the following people:

Adrienne, Beth, Dad, Eli, Gina, Joel, Josh, Lea, Matt, Mia, Michelle, Mom, Phila, Sarah, and all the nice staff at CPL.

"I can do all things through Christ who strengthens me."
– Philippians 4:13

CHAPTER ONE

My life has always been absolutely beautiful. Amazing. Perfect. Floating in the salty ocean, lying on endless sandy beaches, school, surfing, boys, beach parties, night dips. Everything has always been exactly as it should be. Until one day it all came crashing down.

Kinda like I wish this stupid plane would do.

Don't give me that look. You can't just sit there and judge me when you don't even know what I'm going through. Trust me, if you had lived 16 glorious years on the island paradise of everyone's dreams only to be ripped away to the icy cold North, you'd be willing to go down on a plane too.

What's wrong with it? What's *wrong* with it? What *is* wrong with it? Let me paint you a little picture.

Picture yourself—not on a boat on the river—lying on a towel, stretched out on white sands, the sound of the ocean waves calming you as a breeze filters through your salt-tangled hair. The palm trees sway back and forth, offering you occasional shade from the hot rays of light.

As you sunbathe, you become aware of a distinct presence. It's your crush, Kaipo, his golden hair soaked, his bronzed skin practically glowing.

You sit up, trying to look sexy, which is difficult when your breasts

1

haven't quite developed yet. You put on an air of bored interest in an effort to hide the fact that you're re-adjusting the back of your bikini bottoms. Kaipo doesn't seem to notice, but maybe he's just being polite.

He shakes the water out of his hair and finally looks down at you. "Hey," he says coolly with a nod.

You smile and open your mouth, but at first no sound comes out. Then finally:

"Hey."

"Mind if I...?" he gestures to your towel.

"Yeah, sure!" you exclaim a little too enthusiastically.

Then you both sit together in silence, staring out at the waves.

"So, I was thinking—"

"Did you know—?"

You both try to speak at the same time, and then laugh awkwardly as you look away from each other. A moment later, he touches your shoulder.

"Ladies first."

"I was gonna say that—" You get interrupted by the sound of a cell phone ringing. It's yours. Of course.

"Are you gonna answer?" Kaipo asks.

"Nah," you say with a smile. "What were you saying?" you ask because you feel weird now.

He chuckles at your change of topic, but answers anyway. "I was thinking about that new Italian restaurant. And I thought—"

The cell phone rings again and you let out a little frustrated sigh. "Sorry, just go ahead," you tell him.

Kaipo glances down at the sound coming from your bag and raises an eyebrow. "Why don't you just hit ignore so the sound stops?"

You take out your phone and see that your mother is trying to get a hold of you. "Because if I do that, my parents will know I'm purposefully

2

ignoring them. If I let it ring, then I can pretend I didn't hear it."

When he starts to laugh, your face flushes hot. "Not that I'm trying to be dishonest. Usually I would answer, it's just that I know my mom's just calling to tell me dinner will be ready soon."

You stare at the waves again as you wait for the ringing to stop. There are some little kids splashing around in the water, giggling, jumping, and even diving in. It's really cute—if you like children.

When your mom finally gives up, Kaipo turns to you and says smoothly, "Speaking of dinner, I was wondering if…"

"Yeah?" you coax with what you hope is a coy smile.

"Well, I mean…if you're free and all…if you want…" his voice gets all shy, which you find really cute.

Just as you poise your lips to say yes, the phone starts ringing again. You sigh heavily. "I'm sorry, Kaipo," you tell him as you take out your phone.

"It's okay, Elli," he says with a gentle smile. "You should answer it. Tell her that…maybe you won't be home for dinner?"

You grin widely at him and then hit answer on your phone. It's your father this time.

"Elli?" he sounds concerned, but you can't think of why he would be. "We've been trying to get a hold of you."

"Sorry, Dad," you say. "I'm just at the beach with friends." You add the "with friends" because your parents don't like it when you go swimming in the ocean alone. It's kind of true anyway. Kaipo *is* your friend.

"Well, we need you to come home, honey," Dad says. He sounds vaguely urgent, but you're too preoccupied getting lost in Kaipo's sweet blue eyes to care much.

"Um, I kind of have dinner plans," you say. Hastily, you add, "If that's okay."

"It's not," Dad says. "Come home please."

"But Dad—"

"Elikapeka," he says, and you know it just got real serious because he almost never uses your full name. "Your mother and I need to talk with you. Come home."

You swallow back your disappointment, but you know you can't argue. He's serious. He's not even doing it just to ruin the almost-date you had. He really needs you to come home.

"Okay," you say quietly. Casting the briefest of glances at Kaipo, you add, "See you soon."

You look up at Kaipo as you end your call. He says, "So…"

"Hold that thought," you say, trying to sound cool, even though you're mad at your parents. "I have to go home. But just…ask me again soon, okay?"

As you get up, he asks, "Is everything alright?"

You shrug. "Apparently my parents want to talk to me."

"Sounds serious," he teases.

As you head toward your bicycle, you say dryly, "Yeah, maybe they're finally getting a divorce." You immediately regret your comment though, remembering how Kaipo's parents got a divorce just two years ago.

"Oh, Kai," you say, feeling like an idiot. "I'm sorry. I shouldn't have said that."

He shrugs but you know his nonchalance is forced. "Don't worry about it. I'll catch up with you later, Elli."

"Bye," you say as he walks away.

As you pedal home, you wonder if maybe your parents really are getting a divorce this time. It's not like you haven't noticed how much they dislike each other. Were they ever in love? Was the last time they felt love for each other sometime before you were born? Did they fall out of love *because* of you?

You shake it off before you go inside your house. You remind yourself that their problems are not your own. Or at least, that's what you think for a few blissful minutes before you actually sit down with dear, sweet Mommy and Daddy.

When you get inside, you expect there to be some special guest for dinner or something. But instead, it's just Mom and Dad. They stay quiet as they pass you food to put on your plate. You sense something's up, so for once you keep your mouth shut and don't complain about not getting a date with Kaipo.

Finally, as Mom serves up some bowls of ice cream, Dad looks right at you and says, "Elli, we have some big news for you."

You swallow hard as your heart starts hammering in your chest. This is it. You're sure they're breaking up.

"We're moving," he says after what feels like an eternity.

You exhale deeply with relief. You're just moving. They're not breaking up. Everything is still okay. "To where?" you ask, thinking maybe you'll finally get a room with a walk-in closet.

Dad exchanges a look with Mom. He nods his head in your direction like he wants her to do something. In response, she rolls her eyes and takes a big bite of ice cream. He pushes his plate away from himself in a clear display of rejection for her dessert choice, to which she shrugs like she doesn't care even though she really does.

When Dad stalls long enough, Mom says, "Oh, just tell her, Robert."

He gives you a sheepish look and says, "We're moving to Toronto."

You can only think of one Toronto, but you're fairly certain that they couldn't possibly mean *that* one. So you ask hopefully, "That's...near Honolulu, right?" because you can't bear the thought of moving so far away.

"No, Elli," Mom says. "We're going back to Canada."

You look back and forth between your mom and dad and they stare back at you. You start to laugh—out of nervousness and also because you're hoping that they're actually just joking. Finally you realize they're serious.

"*We're* moving back to Canada?" you burst out. "*We* never lived in Canada."

Mom sighs, which is quite possibly the most annoying reaction to you. "Your father and I did. Now we're going back."

"I got transferred," Dad adds, as if this is an acceptable excuse for ruining your life.

Your face heats up and your head spins as you stand suddenly, knocking over your chair. "This is so unfair!" you shout.

Dad winces and Mom gets a steely look in her eyes. You know they're about to reprimand you, so you run to your room and slam the door as hard as you can. The whole house reverberates, but no one calls after you.

The rage calms after a couple of days. During that time, you barely leave your room, you only text your friends to tell them that your life is over, and you don't even answer when Kaipo calls. Your parents give you two weeks to pack up your entire life.

Your friends all come over to help you prepare, and it makes you wonder whether they're being nice or they're just anxious to get rid of you. You go for the former, because it hurts to think about how they'll forget you two weeks after you're gone.

Kaipo comes to see you the day before you leave. You never actually told him you were leaving, but he caught wind of it through a friend of a friend. You sit with him out on the lanai because you don't want your parents to eavesdrop.

"Why didn't you tell me you were leaving?" he asks, sadness in his eyes.

"Because..." you falter. This is your last chance to say something meaningful before you go. So, you gather all your courage and say, "Because I really, really like you, and I just couldn't face it. I don't want to leave this place and I especially don't want to leave you."

He frowns and you're terrified that you've said the wrong thing. Then, in a surprise gesture of romantic-ness, he kisses you. Like a full-on, hands in your hair, tongue against tongue, don't-care-who's-looking kiss. Kai's lips are warm and soft and taste vaguely like the ocean, which isn't half as bad as it sounds.

"I wish we'd had more time, Elli," he says when he finally lets your lips go.

"Me too, Kai," you whisper back.

Then he leaves forever, or rather you leave forever, because the next day you're on a plane bound for Canada in the dead of winter. And you just keep wishing that you'd wake up back in the real world. You keep wishing that Kaipo's kiss had stopped time so that you never had to leave. But it didn't. The stupid plane keeps heading farther and farther north.

Obviously this story is about me, and not you. But you get the idea.

CHAPTER TWO

I sigh for the fifteenth time in ten minutes. Mom's asking me again if I'm settling in okay, if I like the bookshelf, if I want paint for my room, and if I'm ever going to get rid of the boxes. And again I reply that I never plan to settle in, the bookshelf looks like every other bookshelf, I want black paint to symbolize how my life is over, and I'll get rid of the boxes when we move back to Hawaii. Mom scowls—again, I might add—and then leaves my brand-new, horribly cold bedroom.

I look around. There are two things on the bookshelf: dust and a book that the previous owner left behind. The boxes that contain the entire contents of my life—minus the social part that I left in a coffin back in Hawaii—are all stacked up in neat rows along the wall underneath the two big windows. The windows that are extremely drafty, or so it feels. Everything in this freaking country is so freaking cold that I can't understand how anyone could have colonized this place.

I glance at the desk that Dad bought a few days ago. He put it together for me because I couldn't be bothered. It has a lot of little drawers and spots for personal things like pictures and CDs, and would be quite attractive if I weren't so dead inside. I only have my laptop on it and a couple of letters from friends back home. The letter from Kai is on top. Even though I got it yesterday, the envelope is still sealed. I want to read it, but I'm afraid of my heart breaking all over again.

The only clothes I've bothered to unpack are the ones I've been wearing every day. And let me tell you, I learned pretty quickly that absolutely *nothing* I own is appropriate for the weather in the Arctic Tundra. Mom said we'd go shopping really soon, before the next school semester starts. We haven't yet—partially because I can't bring myself to go outside, and partially because Mom and I aren't exactly on good enough terms right now to actually shop together. Still, I know it's unavoidable, no matter how much I want to go home.

Looking outside the window, I still see all that grotesque white stuff falling from huge, dark grey clouds. It reminds me of the ash from burnt sugar cane fields, except that I know it's a lot colder. It has one thing going for it though: it doesn't smell bad. But then, it doesn't smell like anything.

There's nothing interesting in the view outside my window, unless you like snow, snow-covered chimneys, snow-covered roofs, snow-covered street lights…you get the picture. The houses—or what I can see of the houses—are actually kind of cute. They're all red brick, with brown, grey, or black shingles. It's like something out of a movie. I guess I don't mind them, but it's still not home.

There is one thing I really do like, though (that I swear I'll never admit to my parents). You know those street lamps I mentioned? Well, they're just ordinary street lamps and there's nothing special about them. But…a couple of nights ago when I couldn't sleep because of the cold and loneliness, I got up and started pacing. When I passed the window, I caught sight of the light from the lamp glowing down on the snowy roof next to ours. My breath caught in my throat—an involuntary reaction that I despised—and I couldn't tear my gaze away from it.

I had never seen snow before, only in movies, and even then, a camera can't quite do this particular vision justice. The way the smooth-looking snow takes on the colour of the light and then sparkles like a thousand little diamonds? It was…

It was magical. There, I said it.

Other than that small glimmer of light, things here are pretty miserable. Honestly, how can they stand it? It's just so…ugh. Then I have to start school in a few days, and get this: I actually have to *walk*. Like, people actually *walk* in the cold. And from what I can tell, they look about as normal as if they were walking barefoot along a beach. Can you imagine? *How* am I ever going to accomplish walking in this weather while a) not dying and b) looking normal?

*　　　*　　　*

So now I'm out at some mall with Mom, feeling absolutely ridiculous because I'm sure I look like a fool. I mean…I'm wearing about five shirts underneath an old winter coat Mom dredged up from who knows where, and a pair of pyjama bottoms underneath my jeans with running shoes that are soaked through because I don't own any waterproof boots. I feel like everyone in the mall is staring at me, but that's probably because I'm staring at all of them, wondering how anyone could possibly look comfortable in their winter attire.

It's hot in the mall, but it's a fake hot. It makes me sweat under my layers and fools me into believing that it's not really as cold outside as I originally thought. But then I see people bust in through the outer doors, bringing in cold gusts of wind and snow, and I know I'm not imagining this awful winter bitterness.

I hear some giggling to my left, and I turn, expecting to have to give some girls a dirty look for laughing at me. But when I look over, I see they're not actually paying attention to me at all. They're checking out a group of guys who just walked in from outside. I can't see what's so special about them—they're all wearing similar coats and knit hats that cover both sides of their faces, and they all have dorky grins as they nod their heads at the girls.

I sigh at them. Everything is so blah here that I just can't see how they could get enthusiastic about anything, much less the totally unsexy clothing they're hiding under. I'm not saying they should go around in underwear or something—they would surely die if they did. I'm just saying that it must be hard to feel flirty in…in that!

Seriously, *knit* hats? My grandma once sent me a knit hat that I quickly disposed of. Mom sent a very kind letter thanking her on my behalf and made no mention of my real reaction to it. The truth was that we—well *I*— have never actually visited either set of grandparents or anyone in Canada. And I have to say, I'm really not impressed with my first time here.

"Elli," my mother says impatiently.

I turn my focus back to her and it's clear that she's been trying to get my attention for a few minutes. "Sorry?" I say, in a way that means, "Please repeat yourself because I zoned out again."

Mom shakes her head. "What do you think of this store, I said. There might be some nice sweaters."

"Sure, Mom," I say, resigned. What else am I supposed to do? I have to reconstruct my *entire* wardrobe and at this point, I don't even really care whether the sweaters are nice or not.

By the end of the shopping spree, I have ten new sweaters, some fleece-lined jeans, knee-length socks, boots, mittens, gloves, scarves of various colours, a couple of coats, and even one of those hats, although not the kind with the flaps. At first, I was trying to make economic choices, but Mom basically told me to just get whatever I wanted and that Dad's company would cover the credit card charges. I think maybe that was

11

Mom's way of saying sorry for bringing me to the tundra and I can't say I'm not at least a little bit forgiving.

*   *   *

The first day of school is brutal. Mom doesn't make me walk, claiming that it's just so I can learn the route. I think it has more to do with the fact that, after seventeen years, even my Canadian-born mother isn't used to the cold anymore and she felt bad for me. But other than getting a ride in a warm car, the rest of my day is horrible.

I've never been the new kid at school before. But I'm halfway through grade eleven and halfway around the world. This is not fun, it's not comfortable, and it's not cool. I want to say I hate my parents, until I pull the sleeves of my cashmere sweater over my fingers in a gesture of social awkwardness. Cashmere is *so* soft.

All of my teachers, without fail, pronounce my name incorrectly. Most of them pronounce it "A-leek-a-peek-a," which makes all the students laugh. Especially since my chemistry teacher makes it sound like he likes taking a peek. And every single time I correct them, I have to have a lengthy discussion about "what my name means." It's super awkward, especially since it doesn't mean anything other than "when my parents had me, they were obsessed with Hawaiian culture and really it just means Elizabeth, but please just call me 'Elli.'"

See what I mean?

Lunch is lonely. I wasn't super popular back home, but I had my own group of friends. I've never known what it's like to be on the outside until today. I could barely find a spot to sit because I didn't want to be that loser that has to beg a group of people for a spot at their table only to be rejected. It's much easier for everyone if you do the rejection part yourself.

But then a weird thing happens. This random guy sits down, not right next to me or directly across from me, but still close enough that it feels like

12

he's trying to sit *with* me. And like he might get the wrong idea and start a conversation with me.

Okay, that sounds bad, I know. I mean, I'm not an unfriendly person. Normally, I think I'm pretty pleasant to be around. But not today. Today I'm just in a bad mood, the same bad mood I've been in since Mom and Dad said we were moving. So if this guy thinks that he can just sit here and—

"Is that the mystery meat?" he asks, pointing a stubby finger at my plate of cafeteria-issued food. I don't get time to answer before he continues. "Because as a veteran, I feel I should warn you. If they ever offer you the mystery meat," he pauses to smile, "don't be afraid to take it. It's just beef."

I don't know what to say to him. Why is he talking to me? And about beef, of all things? And what's with the serious lack of a tan? Honestly, this guy is so light you'd think the sun didn't even visit Canada. I look around briefly just for comparison's sake. No one else is quite as anti-tanned as him, so I can only assume he's just a weirdo.

"Uhhh," I say finally, realizing that he's just waiting for some kind of an answer. But what exactly does one say to that?

"I know, I know," he says with a little chuckle. "It's scary being in a new school, which is why I thought to tell you that you made a good choice for your meal today. Tomorrow though, they're offering fish sticks. I suggest a bag lunch."

"Th-thanks," I stutter, since I've apparently lost all ability to communicate properly.

He gives me a dorky smile, which, if I weren't in such a bad mood, might have been slightly endearing. As it is, I find it more-than-slightly annoying. I wait until he looks away so I can take a good look at him.

Aside from the anti-tan he's not that bad-looking. He has rectangular glasses that give his otherwise plain-shaped face some definition. There are blue eyes hiding behind thick eyebrows that are a shade darker than his plain brown hair. He's not skinny or built, but he's not fat either. A little on the chubby side, I guess. I watch him write math equations in a notebook, and notice that while his fingers look like they should be clumsy, they actually move quite deftly.

And then it dawns on me. He's a nerd, which explains why he doesn't look athletic or like he fits in with any of the other groupings I see around the cafeteria. It also explains his skin-tone. It's not an anti-tan I'm looking at, but more likely a computer screen tan.

"Ah," I say audibly. *Whoops.*

He raises one of those bushy eyebrows at me. "What?"

"What?" I repeat, my own finely-plucked eyebrows drawing in.

His eyes crinkle in amusement. "You said, 'Ah,'" he says, making a sweeping gesture in the air with his hands.

"I did?" I ask, feigning ignorance.

He nods, clearly trying to hide his grin. "Where exactly are you from, again?"

"I…" I pause. Why am I even bothering? I'm still hoping Dad will find a way to take me back to Hawaii. "I don't think I ever said."

"Ella, is it?" he asks out of the blue.

The bell rings then, saving me from having further conversation with him. "Close enough," I say, grabbing my stuff quickly and attempting to make a hasty exit.

As it turns out, I didn't need to run off so quickly. Anti-Tan happens to be in my next class, which makes that at least two classes we have together. I'm sitting in the far corner of the classroom when he walks in. He smiles at me, terrifying me into thinking he might sit next to me, but instead he sits in the front row.

Good. Let's keep it that way.

*　　*　　*

All in all, it was a pretty horrible first day of school. It's a terrible feeling, being that lonely, not knowing anyone, not knowing anything that anyone's talking about because I'm not from anywhere remotely close to here.

On top of that, I felt ridiculous in what I was wearing. Everyone else dumps their coats in their lockers and for the rest of the day they're all walking around in just jeans and t-shirts. Some of the girls even wear nice flats or regular shoes. Meanwhile, I was wearing layers because Mom told me it's warmer in layers. Yeah, I was pretty warm; in fact, I was so freaking warm that I'm sure every other student could just smell me coming. Maybe that's why I didn't make any friends today.

And no, I do not consider Anti-Tan to be my new friend.

At least I've learned my lesson, though. Wear something cute, put something heavier on top of that, then make sure the cute stuff is showing all day long. Gotcha.

This is going to take a lot of getting used to.

CHAPTER THREE

Have I mentioned yet that we don't actually live in Toronto? We live *outside* of Toronto, in a tiny little town. I have to walk to school because I don't live far enough away for the bus to pick me up. Mom assures me that it's no farther than the distance from our old house to my old school, but it feels ten times worse.

Anyway, Anti-Tan is talking to me again today. It's slightly less annoying now, but only because this has been going on for a couple of days and he doesn't seem to mind that I never actually pay any attention to him. But this… this….

Let me explain "this" to you: Anti-Tan, for whatever reason, has taken some sort of liking to me. (I have a feeling it may have something to do with my very obvious and, I must say, beautiful tan.) And because I don't discourage him, he thinks it's okay to continue this thing that we have, where we eat lunch and he talks and maybe I nod sometimes.

I think at one point, Anti-Tan told me his name, but for the life of me I can't seem to remember it. I may have even told him mine, but he still calls me Ella. Whatever. New country, new school, new…"friends." Might as well have a new name, right?

There's this weird chick who keeps glancing over at us every few minutes. She wears what I'm sure she calls "vintage clothing," uses gigantic "retro" headphones, and has a tattoo of a very thorny rose crawling up her hand. She can't be much older than me, and yet, she has a tattoo. Of thorns. I wonder if that's supposed to mean anything?

Still, a part of me finds it very intriguing that she's *so* interested in me and my anti-tan boy. Wait…no. Not *my* boy. He's not mine.

"Ella?"

I whip my head around to face his four eyes. He has one eyebrow lifted high. I say, "Yes?"

His eyes widen. "You actually…answered me?"

So I forgot momentarily that we're not friends because I don't intend to make friends here, and why are you staring at me like that? "So?" I say out loud. When he doesn't say anything, I ask, "What were you saying?"

He smiles, like an honest-to-goodness, I-can't-believe-you-know-my-name kind of smile. Except I'm not sure I do know his name. "I said, 'That's Cherry.'"

"What's Cherry?" I say, trying to sound annoyed, even though I'm not as annoyed as I'd like to be.

"That girl over there with the cool tattoo," he answers.

"Her name is Cherry?" I ask, more curious and losing my annoyed attitude by the second.

He hesitates. "Maybe… Everyone calls her Cherry. We—well, *they*— assume that she strips at night. It's all rumours though. Anyway, she pretty much always responds to Cherry, if anyone actually talks to her."

"Why doesn't anyone talk to her?" *And why do I care so much again?*

He shrugs and mumbles something that sounds suspiciously like, "Because they're all foolish."

"What?" I ask, leaning in.

He studies my face, his eyes trailing down to the hands I've place on the table as if he's trying to see through me. He clears his throat and says, "People are idiots?" like that's what he meant to say in the first place.

"You can say that again," I mutter.

"Can I ask you a question, Ella?" he asks.

"Only if you call me Elli," I answer.

"Oh, but I thought—" he cuts himself off. "Didn't you say your name was Ella?"

No, you *said that.* I shake my head. "It was a misunderstanding," I offer. Why I'm being so nice to him is beyond me.

"Okay, fine. Elli," he restarts with a smile.

I nod, thinking the conversation's over. But then I remember that he was going to ask me something else. He opens his mouth but just as he does, the bell rings.

"Time for class," I say with a shrug. "Seeya."

"Why don't we just walk together?" he asks, getting up as I do and hefting his full bag over his shoulder.

"What?" I distractedly shove the remains of my lunch back into my bag.

"We have class together," he says, giving me a weird look. "We might as well walk together."

"I have to stop at my locker," I tell him honestly. I'm not trying to get away from him. Well, not just that. I really *do* have to go to my locker. "Don't you?"

He shakes his head slightly with a frown. "I don't use a locker. See you later, Elli."

I want to say "Just wait for me," or "Come to my locker with me," but I don't. I don't know why not. I'm not shy, I don't have trouble talking to guys. But something about the way Anti-Tan said "I don't use a locker," made me stop myself. Maybe he's just a weird kid.

Whatever. I really *don't* want to make friends here.

*   *   *

That weird chick. Cherry. She's walking straight towards me. It's been a few days since I caught her staring at me and Anti-Tan. But now I see her in the hall, and maybe she's not heading towards me, but it certainly *seems* like she is.

And then she's pinning me with her gaze and all doubts as to her intended destination flee my mind. She's got this intense look in her eye and I don't know whether or not I should be afraid, or what I should do at all. So, I just stand there and stare back at her.

Then she reaches me and puts out her hand. "Hi!" she says a little too loudly.

I'm caught off-guard by the volume of her greeting and, startled, I step back a bit.

"Oh, sorry," she says, practically yelling now. She pulls her headphones off and when she does, I can hear a strong beat coming out of them. In a more normal voice, she says, "I always forget how loud I am when I'm listening to music."

I gape at her like I've lost the ability to speak. I don't know what she wants. I don't know what to say to that. I don't even want to be here.

"Anyway," she continues, evidently unruffled by my reaction. "I'm Cherry." Her hand is outstretched again and she pushes it even more towards me and laughs. "Look, I know you're from out of town, but I'm pretty sure shaking hands is a universal thing."

"Oh!" I say. I'm flabbergasted and slightly intimidated, but I shake Cherry's hand anyway. "Is your name really Cherry?"

I'm not usually that rude. I don't ask people why they have the name they have, why their hands are covered in thorny roses, why they're wearing

19

a purple skirt with rainbow tights in the middle of winter, whether they have a loving mother and father at home. But for some reason, I couldn't help just blurting it out.

Fortunately for me, she just laughs. "My dad picked the name. You'd think my mom was a stripper or something, but no. He just really likes cherries. I think if I'd been a boy he would have still called me Cherry. Weird, eh?"

Eh? *Eh?* I'd heard about this peculiar little Canadian expression, but I thought it was like leprechauns and fairies and didn't really exist.

Cherry's still talking. "So, anyway, what's your name?"

"Elikapeka," I respond.

Cherry laughs harder this time. "And you think my name is weird? Do people call you that, like, all the time?"

"Umm..." I'm too shocked at her rudeness to think straight. "Not really," I finally respond. "My friends usually call me Elli."

"Ella totally suits you," she says, clasping her hands dramatically in front of her.

What is it with people and calling me Ella? How does the "ee" sound turn into the "uh" sound? That doesn't make any sense. But there's nothing I can do about it now because Cherry is saying my new name over and over with different inflections...

"Ella! *Ella.* El*la?* Well, that one was kind of weird." What is she even going on about? "Anyway, cool name."

"You too," I say lamely.

Cherry suddenly turns serious. "Hey, soo...what's the deal with you and Jules?"

"Jules?" I ask, perplexed.

"Yeah. Julian VanderNeen," she says. She makes Os with her hands and puts them up to her eyes. "Thick glasses, thick skin, almost no colour to speak of…"

Oh. So that's his name. It's prettier than I remembered it being. But then, I don't think I remembered it at all. "Oh, yeah. Umm. There's no deal."

"*Really?*" she asked. "Because…"

"What?" I persist when she stops speaking. What does she care about me and Anti—I mean Julian?

"You know what?" Cherry says, lifting a finger in the air. Then she smiles. "Never mind. Look, I'll see you around, okay?"

"O-okay," I stammer. Cherry's introduction of herself and Julian has left me completely speechless.

*   *   *

I've come home to a screaming match. And I really do mean it when I say that. My mother is an excellent screamer, but my father… If the man had a woman's voice, he'd be able to best Mom. I don't even know what they're arguing about, but within a few minutes I hear things about my grandparents, my dad's "weird" brother, and the state of their finances.

You should know that my parents have never been in any kind of financial distress. I know most kids assume their parents just have everything like that under control, but I *know* for a fact that they're pretty well-off. And yet, they always manage to bring money into their fights. It boggles my mind, but I've gotten pretty used to ignoring them.

I find myself suddenly wishing for a pair of Cherry's headphones. That way I could drown out everything else and if I absolutely had to speak, I could yell and get away with it. It'd be great.

I immerse myself in a book that has nothing to do with school. I *should* be doing homework, but I just can't bring myself to actually get it out and do it. I've always been a straight-A student and while I still pretty much hate it here, I would probably hate losing that, too. Still, homework today is just so…blah. Especially when it's Canadian history. Like, honestly, people actually study that. I mean, it's not like—

"Elli!" Mom and Dad both yell at the same time.

I groan audibly to no use. They can't hear it, so my passive-aggressive display of displeasure is lost on them. I want to ignore them, but I know I can't. I just don't want to feel like they're dragging me into their disagreement.

"What?" I say begrudgingly as soon as I step into the living room where they're waiting for me.

"We have some news," Mom says, clearly taking charge over Dad. "Big news."

I put on a fake smile and practically shout, "We're moving back?!"

Dad shakes his head while Mom rolls her eyes. Dad says, "No, Elli. We're not. Sorry , kiddo."

Kiddo. I snort. "Then there's nothing more I really need to hear," I say, boldly defying my parents.

And with that, I leave the room and bound up the stairs. In reality, I do want to hear what my parents have to tell me, considering last time they used that tone of voice they dropped a bomb. But at the same time, I want them to suffer for the way they're making me suffer.

*   *   *

The next morning, I head downstairs for my customary bowl of cereal. I normally do this before I shower, so of course my hair is completely mussed up and I'm in my "comfy" pyjamas. When I reach the kitchen and see a man in his late twenties sitting at the table and reading a newspaper, I can't help but scream at the top of my lungs.

He looks up startled, like I'm the one intruding, and I panic. I'm freaking out and I don't know what to do. So I grab the closest thing to me—the frying pan that he must have used to make the eggs he's eating.

Ugh, who breaks into a house at 7:30 in the morning to eat someone else's eggs?

I hear heavy footsteps coming down the stairs and I hope to God it's my dad. I'm still holding the frying pan like Rapunzel, aiming it toward the stranger without getting too close.

"Elli," Dad says with a relieved sigh when he finally reaches the kitchen.

"Call 9-1-1," I say frantically, not taking my eyes off of the strange man.

Then my dad does something completely unexpected and perplexing. He starts to laugh like I haven't heard him laugh in years. And not only that, but the man at the table also laughs.

"Dad!" I exclaim, whirling around to face him.

Dad wipes the laughter from his face as he gently takes the frying pan out of my iron grip. He wraps an arm around my shoulders and turns me back around to face the stranger.

"Elli, meet your Uncle Daniel," Dad says with some mirth left in his voice. "He's going to be staying with us for a while."

I sigh in relief and all the tension leaves my body. It occurs to me then that this must have been what they were fighting about last night. And then Dad's words sink in and I realize I have to share my house with an uncle I've never met before.

"You have *got* to be kidding me," I say rudely.

Uncle Daniel lifts an eyebrow—he looks just like my Dad, how did I miss that?—and says, "Nice to meet you too, Elli."

CHAPTER FOUR

"Actually," Uncle Daniel continues, "we've met before. But you were like two years old. And I was mostly drunk."

I flounder around for useless words as Dad grabs a bowl and starts mixing himself some cold cereal. Finally, I say, "I'm sorry I screamed at you."

"I'm sorry I scared you," Uncle Daniel says kindly, and I think I might even want to like him at that moment. Then he frowns. "But didn't you know I would be here?"

"She seems to have missed that information somehow," Dad says oh-so-helpfully.

I roll my eyes at him and look back at my unfamiliar uncle. When I first saw him he seemed like a regular guy, albeit a break-and-enter kind. But now I'm seeing some similarities to my dad. He's got the same sandy brown hair, the same hazel-green eyes, and the same chin. But the sassy little smirk he's giving me isn't shared with Dad.

He's got laugh lines that crinkle the corners of his eyes and a five o'clock shadow that makes me think that maybe he's a little older than my earlier assessment. In truth, I don't know that much about my father's only brother, but I'm under the impression that there's a very good reason for that.

And that reason is striding into the kitchen, already dressed in a classy business suit, with her hair perfectly coiffed. Ugh, she even has heels on. Isn't it too early for heels?

"Morning, Elli," she says to me.

"Hi, Mom," I say. I'm still trying to calm my heart from the near heart attack I just suffered and I'm hoping she'll make me some breakfast.

No dice. She turns a fake smile to my uncle, but I know what that look really means. "Daniel…nice to see you again. You must have gotten in *quite* late last night."

"Shauna," Uncle Daniel says as he rises.

He goes over to her and makes the mistake of trying to give her a hug. I honestly don't think my mom will accept a hug from anyone anymore. Except me, of course. She raises an eyebrow and narrowly escapes his awkward attempt at estranged affection. He handles it well though and sits back down with another smirkish smile. I'm almost impressed that he can shake her attitude off so easily.

"So, um," I start to say, but Mom cuts me off before I can get any further.

"Well, Elli," she says, starting to answer the question I didn't ask, "if you would just listen to us once in a while you'd know exactly what your—" she spits out the next word, "—*uncle* is doing here."

"Dad already told me," I say, trying not to sound like a defiant brat. It's hard to be taken seriously with a certain tone of voice. "And I was going to say…" *think of something else, anything to break this tension,* "does anyone want to take me to the mall after school?"

It's not what I meant to say, but I figure no one will volun—

"I will," Uncle Daniel says suddenly.

25

My dad frowns in a pensive way and my mom huffs like she can't believe he would offer such a thing. But since neither of my parents is saying anything and since I was dumb enough to ask in the first place, I can't exactly refuse.

"O-okay," I manage to say.

"Cool," he says. "Pick you up after school."

"Do you even own a vehicle?" Mom asks rudely. Now I know where I get it from.

"How do you think I got here?" my uncle says boldly. "I mean, this house isn't exactly on a bus route, and I don't feel like shelling out taxi money, soo…"

He leaves his sentence hanging as Mom rushes to the front room to look out the window. I can hear her exaggerated gasp from two rooms away. "Daniel!" she cries, clicking her way back to the kitchen. "You are not taking my daughter anywhere in that rusty old bucket of bolts."

"Shauna," Dad groans. "Would you relax? She's my daughter, too, and it's my brother taking her."

"You can't possibly be serious," Mom says to him. "You want to let Elli ride around with your brother in—in that?"

"It's not like he's reckless," Dad says. "They'll be fine."

"I'm right here," I say, exasperated. I'm surprised to find the exact same words being said an octave lower at the same time. Uncle Daniel is clearly as irritated with them as I am.

I don't know the guy, but I already feel bad for him. I say, "I have to go get ready for school. But I'll see you later?"

"Sure, Elli," he says, almost sighing.

*   *   *

I didn't really expect my uncle to take me to the mall, especially since I never even told him what school I go to. But to my surprise, as soon as I step out of the front doors, there he is. The car is unmistakable—what my mother called a "bucket of bolts" I would call "slightly rusted," but I guess that's a matter of opinion. I gape at the car for all of five seconds before Uncle Daniel honks at me.

Something in me snaps and I laugh because the horn sounds like a toy car instead of a real car. I go over and hesitate before getting in, but then the cold gets too much for me.

"You look surprised to see me," Uncle Daniel says as he starts driving—at a reasonable pace, I might add.

I decide to be honest with him. "I didn't actually think you would want to go to the mall with me."

"I didn't think you'd want to go with your parents," he says. With another one of his classic smirks, he adds, "I mean, I know I'm old, but they're…really old."

I laugh, mostly for his sake. "Well, I only said I wanted to go to the mall to have something to say. That whole scene at breakfast…"

"Yeah." He nods and he even looks a little sad. "How long have they been like that?"

I pause before answering quietly, "A long time. I think they fell out of love when I started growing up."

I didn't really mean to say it, but it's too late to take it back. I know Uncle Daniel heard me because he gives me this look, brief enough to concentrate on his driving but long enough for me to know what he means by it. Pity, is what he's trying to communicate. Well, I don't want any of that.

"Look, it's really okay," I tell him. "When they're focused on each other, they leave me alone." This time, he shoots me a worried look. "No, no it's great! Trust me."

"It's not that…" he says, letting his sentence trail off. Then he shrugs.

"Well, not completely."

"Then what?" I ask.

I watch as Uncle Daniel hesitates, clearly trying not to show how hard he's thinking about my question. He finds a good excuse for not answering as he parks the car in a cramped space of the overcrowded parking lot. When he very meticulously starts rearranging things on his person before actually turning the car off, that's when I get impatient.

"What?" I persist, sounding whinier than I mean to sound. He still doesn't answer. "Uncle Daniel, what are you trying so hard not to tell me?"

He shrugs again in a careless way that actually makes me want to shake him. "It's just…" he turns to me. "They used to be so in love. Like, sickeningly in love. You know, the way that makes everyone else feel uncomfortable because it's so…sweet?"

My eyes must look like two big, blue saucers to him. I know what he's talking about but my parents haven't been like that in a long time.

"Anyway, it's none of my business," he states as he reaches for the handle.

Taking his cue, I also get out of the car. He starts to walk ahead of me and I follow him, assuming that he's leading me somewhere.

Then he says over his shoulder, "Meet back at the car in like, an hour? Is that long enough for you?"

I stop in my tracks, but he doesn't notice because he's hurrying toward the door. So, he doesn't actually want to hang out with me. I know I should have seen that coming, and to be honest we don't even know each other, so it really shouldn't quite hurt like it does. I swallow down his seemingly careless rejection and also hurry into the super-heated mall. I just hope that I'll be able to find my way out to the car in an hour.

Not quite knowing what to do with myself—because I didn't really need to come to the mall in the first place—I wander aimlessly. I recognize a bunch of the stores from having come here a couple of times with Mom, but other than that I feel completely out of place. Although, these days, out of place is starting to feel normal.

I have this paranoid feeling of being watched by everyone I pass by. I wonder if maybe they can tell I'm foreign somehow, like my skin tone gives me away. But I see their faces, and I know their fake tans look as good as my real one. So what is it that gives me away? Maybe it's just me. Maybe I'm giving off some sort of hormonal scent that sets me apart.

Maybe I'm just crazy and no one is really taking any special notice of me. I look to my left where a giggling group of girls is making their way into one of those glitzy but cheap jewellery stores and am assaulted by the completely opposite feeling of being completely ignored. This, of course, proves to be my downfall, as I walk straight into the broad chest of a boy I vaguely recognize as being in my chemistry class.

"Oof," he mutters as he draws back a bit.

"I'm so sorry," I say quickly, trying to conceal my gasp of delighted surprise when I see how much more handsome he is when I'm not running into him. He has dark, curly hair and warm, chocolate brown eyes that are searching my face. If Kai, with his sun-streaked blond hair and ice blue eyes, is day, then this guy is night. Not that there's anything particularly wrong with that.

"Sorry," he drawls very slowly, an expression on his face that verges on amusement. With a twitch of his lips, he repeats the word "sorry," but it sounds more like he's saying "sore-y."

I open my mouth to speak, but out comes his voice saying, "Aren't you that girl from, umm…Alaska, or something?"

I start and choke out, "*Hawaii.*"

"I was so close," he deadpans, and he's so good at it that I can't even tell if he's joking or not. Then his face cracks into the dimpliest grin I've ever seen.

He turns his head slightly and I see that there's actually a group of boys that he's hanging out with and now they're calling his name. It's Adrian.

"See you later, Hawaii," Adrian says just before he swings back around and walks away from me with his friends.

I go back to my wandering around, only now I'm also trying to get Adrian's face—and his gorgeous name—out of my head. When the time comes for me to meet Uncle Daniel back at the car, I realize that I actually haven't done anything productive or remotely useful here. Figuring that my uncle probably won't like the idea of his coming out here in vain, I pop into a clothing store on my way toward the exit and buy the first shirt I see that's on sale. It's not much, but it'll do.

I head out to the still-crowded parking lot and for the life of me, I cannot remember what Uncle Daniel's bucket of bolts looks like. My saving grace is that Uncle Daniel himself is standing outside his car, leaning against it actually, and sipping some hot liquid through a Tim Horton's travel cup. I shiver inside my heavy coat just *thinking* about how long he could have possibly been waiting outside like that for me. His coat isn't even done up, but at least he has a grey scarf, albeit a ratty one, wrapped around his neck.

"Have you been waiting long?" I ask him. Up close, I see that the reason his coat isn't done up is because all but one of the buttons are missing.

He turns to me with a smile and shakes his head. "Nope."

"Why didn't you wait inside? You could have turned the car on," I say.

He unlocks my door for me and then holds it open. "I don't like to idle," he says simply. "Plus it's nice out."

I shiver. "I didn't really have you down for the environmental type," I joke as I slip inside the car.

"I'm not," he says as he gets in on his side. "I'm just cheap."

He smirks at me and I laugh. I think I'm going to like having my uncle around.

CHAPTER FIVE

Julian's giving me a geography lesson. I mean, not just general geography, like where the US is situated in relation to Canada. No, he's giving me the geography of this little tiny town. When it became evident that I had very little knowledge of any of the landmarks in town, he actually took out graph paper and started to draw me a map.

"See?" he says, pointing down at his very meticulous drawing. "The mall's not that far from the school. So you could walk there, rather than have your weird uncle take you there."

Yeah, I told him the whole thing about my uncle and my parents arguing over it. I hadn't really meant to, but it sort of popped up. And let's face it—the only other people I know here are my parents, and I can't really talk to them about, well, them. So I told Julian. He was very sympathetic, even mentioning something about having a strange family, too. For the record, though, he was the one that attributed the adjective "weird" to my uncle.

I shiver, even though it's quite warm inside the school. "Walk to the mall in this weather? No, thanks."

Julian wrinkles his nose, which actually makes his face look kinda cute.

If you're into the geeky type. Which I'm not.

"Oh boy," he says with laughter in his voice. "You're not going to survive the rest of the winter are you?"

I open my mouth to defend myself, which I realize is useless, but instead he keeps going.

"I can see it now." He waves his hand in front of himself like he's imagining some scene playing before him. "The school paper with a gorgeous picture of you on the front page; a headline that reads, 'Ella, who died because she couldn't survive five minutes in the cold.' We'll all show up for the memorial, even though most of the students here don't know you, and we'll light a fire to symbolize the passing of our very own Hawaiian princess. Of course, I'll be the only one who mourns you, because you're the only person with a tan in the wintertime who would even consider hanging out with me."

He chuckles and I can't help myself, even though I don't know why he's still calling me Ella. While I'm flattered by the words 'gorgeous' and 'princess,' I find myself actually laughing at Julian's description. I had no idea he would have that kind of imagination. Then again, I really don't know him that well.

"Or…" he looks under the table for a brief moment and then back at me. "You can buy a more sensible pair of boots, a thick scarf, and a decent pair of gloves."

I snort at the mental image of me, bundled up in all kinds of heavy fabrics, knit things, and ugly boots that go up to my knees. "I'd rather look good than be ridiculously over-dressed."

Julian stares at me for a moment and then says, "Okay the new headline for your obituary now reads: 'Ella, who died in vanity.'"

I'm laughing again, harder this time. While my inevitable death doesn't particularly thrill me, I find Julian's sarcasm hilarious. Who knew a nerdy guy could be so funny?

"No, seriously," I say, trying to catch my breath.

"I *am* being serious," he says, though there's a smile behind those words. "Okay, look. Even I know I'm the last person to be giving fashion advice, but just take a look around. There's not a single girl in this cafeteria whose boots aren't stylish *and* functional. Well, except maybe…" He glances across the room and then quickly looks down at the table. "Cherry's. Everyone knows rubber boots are worn in the springtime. And yet, she always wears hers."

I glance over to where Cherry is sitting alone, quietly reading a book that looks like it's not on the syllabus. I want to comment on how Julian always seems to know things about her, but instead I say, "Rubber boots? For reals?"

"Yes, for reals," he responds dryly. "Would I lie to you?"

I shrug. "How would I know? We haven't known each other that long."

He smiles and his little blue eyes sparkle behind his glasses. "Good point. But I'm not a liar. You'll just have to take my word for it."

I chuckle and find that maybe I don't mind Julian as much as I thought I would. "She asked about you yesterday."

"What?" he asks distractedly as he reaches into his bag to pull out a textbook. It annoys me that he likes to get a head start on homework at lunchtime, but since he is the only almost-friend I have, I don't want to offend him by saying so.

"Cherry," I offer and his head snaps up. "She was asking me about you. I think she thought we were a couple. Which we aren't." I thought I would make that clear, just in case.

Julian's face flushes pink and I think he might actually faint from the exertion of it. "Sorry," I apologize hastily. I grab my hair and start twisting it like I do whenever I feel uncomfortable. "I didn't really mean that the way it came out."

"It's all right, Ella," he says, returning his attention to the textbook. "You and I barely know each other. That's not what I was—" he cuts himself off, chewing on his lip like he's trying hard not to say something.

"That's not what you...?" I prompt, finding myself interested now that I know he's maybe got a secret.

He clears his throat, never once looking at me as he flips through the book. I know his book isn't that fascinating, not even for a geek. When it's clear that he's flipping for the sake of stalling rather than looking for an actual page, I grab it from him and shut it with a satisfying clunk.

"That's not what you were what?" I insist. I guess I've always been a curious person, but normally I'm used to people just telling me things.

Julian sighs. "That's not what I was...you know..." he gestures to his face, which has gone back to its natural non-colour. With a shrug he says, "Look, I know I'm an open book. I'm too honest for my own good and my face tells everything I'm feeling. I'm not that hard to figure out."

"Ah," I say, sort of, kind of getting it. "I have to say, it's interesting to see your face with so much colour. So what were you blushing about anyway?"

His face rouges again. I'm starting to find it rather cute. "It's just Cherry. She's..." he stops then and suddenly rolls his head backwards until he's staring at the ceiling. He lets out an unintelligible groan and asks, "Are you really going to make me say all this?"

Now we're getting somewhere. Excited at the prospect that maybe there's something going on between Jules and Cherry, I try to contain my giggle and say a little too enthusiastically, "Yes!"

As Jules drops his head back down, I catch the tail end of an eye roll. "It's not what you think, Ella."

I just stare at him, a technique which mysteriously seems to work. "Okay. Okay…Cherry and I once had a date." My eyebrows shoot to the ceiling which causes Julian to look a little embarrassed. "Or rather, I should say we were supposed to go on a date. But…I didn't show up."

"What?" I ask. That's not what I was expecting to hear. "Why not?"

He hesitates. "It's complicated."

"How complicated?" I ask him. Now I'm really into this story and I just want to know everything.

"Too complicated to tell you right now," he says. I'm disappointed, but it leaves me hopeful until he says, "Or maybe ever."

"Aw, come on, Jules. Are we friends or not?"

"I just…I don't want to talk about it," he says quietly.

I know he really means it. Like he said himself, he's much too honest for his own good. So I decide to leave him alone about it. But then I think that maybe I'll ask Cherry about it later and wonder if that would be betraying any kind of trust Julian has in me. I put it to the back of my mind, where I can take it out later on my own time and examine it.

"Ella, do you have any idea how often you zone out?" Jules is asking me with an amused tone in his voice. "Because you do it a lot, and frankly it's starting to concern me."

"I'm sorry," I say, with real sincerity in my voice. Maybe I am getting a hang of this whole being Canadian thing.

"Okay, I wasn't going to say anything," Jules changes the subject suddenly, "but Adrian McDuff keeps looking over at you."

"Huh?" I say, oh-so-intelligently.

"Adrian McEveryone-Loves-Me-Just-Because-Duff," Julian says with an exasperated tone.

Jules nods towards a spot behind my right shoulder and I turn to look. There, very openly staring as Jules said, is the boy I ran into at the mall.

Then I remember the name and how I heard one of his friends say it. And of course, he's watching us watching him, so now he knows that we're talking about him. I turn back around before my blush is fully noticeable.

"Oh no, not you, too!" Jules says with exaggerated sorrow in his voice.

That brings me back to Earth and I roll my eyes. "It's not like that. I don't like him. It's just that I literally ran into him at the mall the other day and it was really awkward."

"Literally literally, or figuratively literally?" he asks.

"Literally, as in full on chest bumping," I answer.

Julian not-so-subtly glances down past my collarbone and I lean across the table and whack him on the side of the head.

"Ow," he complains, rubbing his head.

"Didn't your mother ever teach you to respect girls?" I ask in a stern voice, though inside I'm laughing at Julian.

"Sorry," he says sheepishly. Then he shrugs. "I'm just saying, you must have made quite an impression on him."

I roll my eyes. "Okay, can we stop talking about whatever-his-name-is now?"

Julian opens his mouth and I know he's got some witty retort for me, but then the bell rings. I audibly let out a sigh of relief I didn't realize I'd been holding in.

"See you in class, Ella," Jules says as he picks up his bag.

I frown and ask, "Why don't we just walk together?"

Julian hesitates as he watches the other students leave the cafeteria. "Don't you have to go to your locker?"

"Yeah, but I'll be quick," I say. "Come on." If he insists on being friends with me then I figure he might as well accompany me between classes. It's only fair.

Julian pauses, hunches his shoulders, inhales deeply, and then finally says, "'Kay."

I have no idea what his problem is, but he doesn't say another word as he follows me to my locker. When we get to my locker, I open my mouth to say something. But just as the word forms on my lips, Julian is suddenly propelled against the locker next to mine. I turn quickly enough to realize it's because some meathead has pushed him hard.

"Hey!" I yell at the guy, but he completely ignores me. "Are you all right?" I ask Jules.

"Yeah, I'm fine," he says. He doesn't look visibly shaken and his tone of voice is neutral, but I'm sure that what just happened is not fine.

"Really? Because—"

"Don't worry about it, Elli," Jules cuts me off with a shake of his head. He puts a smile on his face, but it's not real and we both know it. But I let it go. Because, again, I don't want offend my new almost-friend.

As we make our way to class, we pass by Adrian McWhat's-His-Name who is *still* staring at us, as if that were his whole aim in life. I frown discouragingly at him and to my dismay, he gives me an alarmingly gorgeous smile back. I look away quickly in case he can tell how hard my heart is suddenly beating.

CHAPTER SIX

Mom and Dad have been fighting more often lately. I can't tell if it's because of the weather, because of my—admittedly rarely-seen—uncle, or because they've basically gotten over each other. I've ruled out that it's me, since they seem to have forgotten that I exist. I guess it's easier to shut them out when they don't pay any attention to me, but it's still disturbing how much more they're fighting. I blame Canada.

It's Saturday and I've spent most of it doing homework. That much has not changed since the big move: teachers here still show their resentment for their jobs by piling homework onto the backs of poor, defenseless students. While I do my math, I can't help but think about Julian, which is totally weird, so I'm glad there isn't much left to do.

I've decided it's time for a break, so I let my laptop boot up while I make myself a snack. I open up my email and gasp when I see an email from Kai. He titled it "So far, so cold," which actually warms my heart.

"Elli," it reads, "I miss you so much! How are you? I can't believe you've been gone for a month already. I keep expecting to see you at school or the beach, but I never do. Obviously.

"I know we haven't really talked about it a whole lot, but our kiss meant a lot to me. I've liked you for a long time and never had the guts to tell you until it was too late.

"I'm sorry, Elli. I'm sorry I was too late and I'm sorry we're so far apart now. I don't know what else to say."

Okay, so, short of proposing, this was probably the best thing he could have ever written me. Like—look at all the beautiful words! My heart aches a little (a lot) at the loss of something I barely even had, and I have to blink several times to keep any tears from falling. I'm afraid to cry in this country because I don't want my tears to freeze.

I start to type out the perfect response to his email. I want to tell him something meaningful, something hopeful, without lying. But it's hard to sound happy when you're completely miserable. Especially since now, I'm reminded of the only kiss I've ever had and that I'll probably never get any more from Kai.

"Kai, I can't believe it's been that long either. Although, it feels a lot longer. How am I doing? Well, it's freezing cold here and I miss you and the gang a lot, but I'm okay." A couple little white lies among the truth can't hurt.

"I can't stop thinking about the way you kissed me before I left. It was the best day of my life, and it probably always will be." Too much? Probably. "I really just wish I could come back and stay forever. Someday, I hope I will.

"Thanks for your email, Kai. It brought a little of that Hawaiian sunshine into my life. Bye for now."

I don't give myself time to edit or even proofread, because I don't want to second-guess myself. Otherwise, I might never send it.

When I'm done rereading Kai's email fifteen times over, I go back downstairs. Mom and Dad are still arguing, but to a lesser degree. Right now, instead of yelling, they're just muttering things at each other. Or maybe they're talking to themselves.

It's none of my business really, so I barge into the den and announce, "I want to go back to Hawaii."

They both stop their ranting to look at me. Mom's face is a mixture of exasperation and surprise; Dad's pity and impatience. They never take me seriously.

When neither of them speaks, I add, "Even just for a little while. Just until winter's over. I can stay at a friend's house."

"That's not happening, Elli," Mom says sternly.

"Why not?" I whine.

"Uh, are you forgetting you have a school to attend? Obligations here at home?" Mom's irritation is quickly turning south. I should have known better than to have this conversation when they were in a bad mood to start with.

I bite back a retort about my so-called obligations at home. I don't do anything at home that would require me to stay in this country. I look at Dad to see if he'll offer me any sort of support, but he avoids my eyes like he'll turn to stone or something.

"This isn't fair," I say. "You know that right?"

Mom sighs. "You've only told us a hundred times."

My fists clench up. What did I do to deserve this treatment from her? I've always been on her side with everything. And now she's throwing my words in my face?

I turn to go just as Dad says, "Shauna. She's just a kid."

"What am I supposed to say to her?" Mom snaps. "We don't have the money to send her back to Hawaii even if I thought that was a good idea."

They don't have money? How much could it possibly cost to go to Hawaii?

"If I get the money myself, can I go back?" I ask, hope running rampant through my veins and out my mouth.

Mom opens her lips and I know she's starting to form the word no. Then Dad, who is now my superhero, says, "Not during school. But maybe…maybe during Spring break. Or after school's done."

"Bob!" Mom exclaims.

"What?" Dad turns on her. "Lots of kids go away for Spring break. And it's not like there aren't a lot of people back home who wouldn't take her for a week."

"Really?!" I squeak. I rush over to my dad and put my arms tightly around his neck. I'm probably suffocating him, but he doesn't seem to care. "Oh, Dad, you're the best!"

"Okay, Elli, okay," he says, gently pulling me back away from him. "But you can only go if you get the money yourself. And it's not cheap to fly to Hawaii."

"I'll get a one-way, then," I say coyly.

Mom's not happy with any of this. "If you can earn enough money for a *return* ticket, then I suppose you can go." Of course she'd say that. There's no way she'd let my dad take all the glory for making me happy.

"Thank you, Mom," I say, offering her a hug too. She doesn't return it, and I'm still not sure why she's so upset.

"I don't know how you're going to get enough money by March…" she warns.

"Yeah, well, I'll try my hardest," I say, grinning at her. She can't keep me down, not now that they've agreed to let me go back. And besides, who says I'll come back when I leave? Wouldn't my parents just love to get rid of me? We'd all be happy, if you ask me.

I go back to my bedroom, happier than I've been since we moved. I wish I could call Kai right now and tell him I'm coming to him. And Sarah, Andrea, Lily… Oh, they'll be so excited to hear.

I'm so elated that I haven't given myself time to think about how exactly I'm going to get the money to go. I don't want to ruin my mood, but it's a valid point my mother made. I can't go if I don't have the money. I also can't go during school and I can't go indefinitely.

I go back online to see what kind of prices a return ticket to Honolulu costs. It's only…$600-800. Okay, breathe, Elli. Next, I look for any community boards that have job postings. Maybe there will be something for me. Of course, my search starts out optimistic and goes downhill from there.

There's *nothing*. I mean, there are some things but unless I have five years' experience, a driver's license, or want to work a night shift at a factory, there's nothing. Not even one single babysitting or dog walking job (not that I'd walk a dog in *this* weather). Ugh.

Sighing, I close my laptop. But I haven't resigned myself to the cold icy North just yet. I will find a way. I just need to look harder. Maybe I can ask at the school office or something.

*   *   *

When I go to school the next day, I make sure to arrive early so I can go into the guidance office. When I go in, the secretary greets me cheerfully. She's an elderly lady who's wearing glasses that, I kid you not, are on a chain. People seriously still wear those. I ask to see a guidance counsellor and she asks if I have an appointment.

"Um, do I need one?" I ask, shifting my backpack nervously.

"Yes, you always need to make an appointment to see the guidance counsellor," she says. "I can pencil you in for next week."

Pencil me in? Who even uses that expression? I mean, she's got a computer *right* in front of her. I choke down my attitude and paste a pleasant smile on my face.

"I'm really just wondering if anyone around here can help me find a job," I tell her, hoping against hope that she'll actually do something for me.

"Oh," she says, surprised. "Well, you don't need to see Mr. Taggart for that. There's a board just outside the office with some flyers. There may be something there. You can also check some of the local stores. There's usually something posted."

I smile again, this time genuinely. Taking a look at the nameplate on the desk, I say, "Thank you, Ms. Robertson."

"You're welcome, dear," she says. She grimaces at me. Or maybe it's a smile. Hard to tell sometimes when people get to a certain age, but at least I know I've maybe found an ally in her.

I go back out and locate the board that's outside. It's encased in glass, as if someone's going to destroy it or something. Or maybe that's happened in the past and they just didn't like it. Whatever the reason, if I want to have any of that information I'll have to write it down or take a picture of it. I opt for taking a picture and pull my phone out in anticipation of several job offers.

There are so many different types of posters—upcoming school events, volunteer opportunities, a flashy green poster calling for auditions for some band, job postings. I see a couple of ads that look promising, even if they won't be terribly well-paying. I take pictures of all of them. Another ad catches my eye. I can't say why exactly, since it has nothing to do with working and is all about the school boxing team. Probably because it's huge and has a picture of a really buff boxer on it. I'm kind of surprised they have a boxing team here, actually.

"Huh," I say, touching the glass where the boxing ad is.

"You're into boxing?" a female voice says over my shoulder.

I turn and find Cherry right next to me. I haven't talked to her since last week, and now I can't help but notice the rain boots. Also, her hair is pink now and it startles me at first. Then I decide it looks kinda good on her and offsets her green eyes nicely. I really want to know how it is that Jules and Cherry ended up with a date together.

"No, not really," I say. "I just thought it was…interesting that your school has a boxing team."

Cherry lets out a guttural laugh. "Oh, it's more than that. They're obsessed with boxing here. Probably because it's the most violent administration-sanctioned activity they can get away with at a school. Our team almost always wins in those big competitions. Not that I keep up with that kind of stuff." She shrugs.

"That's alright." I look at her again, taking in the bright hair, red lips, and dark eye makeup. She's actually kind of pretty; she really makes her style work. "Your hair is pink," I say. I should have complimented it, I can see by the look on her face.

"Yeah, it is." She reaches up and touches her short spiky hair. She seems self-conscious.

"I like it," I say with a smile.

Her eyes flash in a way that makes me glad I told her that. "Thanks. So what are you really doing here? No one actually reads this stuff." She gestures to the board.

"I'm looking for a job," I admit. "See, I want to go back to Hawaii, and I can, if I can get the money for the plane ticket, but I need a job to do that, and well…"

"There's not much, eh?" she says. She studies me for a second then says, "So you're escaping us, are you?"

"What?" I ask. Then I realize she's referring to what I said. "Oh! No. I mean, I'm only supposed to go for a visit. I can't really *leave* leave."

Cherry half-smiles at me. "You don't owe me an explanation. If I could leave for a place like Hawaii, I'd never want to come back."

A crazy thought crosses my mind that almost makes me want to invite her to come, too. But I don't even know her that well and that would be weird. So I don't say anything.

"I think I can help you out though," she's still saying. "My parents own, like, a thing, and I can get you a job there if you want."

A thrill of excitement runs through me, but I'm a little put off by her wording. "What kind of a thing do they own?"

"It's a…okay, well it's the skating rink downtown," Cherry says, putting her hands into her pockets like she's embarrassed. "I didn't want to tell you because you don't seem like you're a big fan of ice. But like, I can get you a job at the snack vending place. Sometimes you get tips."

"Really?" I say, my voice high-pitched with the excitement of it.

"Yeah sure," Cherry says, surprised and slightly amused at my reaction.

"Why would you do that for me?" I ask. I don't mean to sound sceptical, but as soon as I say it, I realize how it could come off.

Cherry shrugs. I'm starting to get that this is her catch-all response. "Because…that's how you make friends, right? By doing nice things for other people."

Her answer catches me off-guard. I'd never really thought of it, but I guess the fact that Julian and Cherry out of all the people here at this school are the only ones who bother with me is pretty awesome. And that's just their way of being a friend to me. Why, I don't know, but I'd rather not question it.

"Thanks, Cherry, I would really appreciate that," I say.

She winks, and then the bell rings and she's gone. Maybe I should invite her to Hawaii after all.

CHAPTER SEVEN

True to her word, Cherry got me a job and now I'm the new snack girl at the skating rink. Which is totally weird. I mean, I've had jobs before, even one scooping ice cream on a beach. But like, people actually willingly come to this frozen *indoor* place for entertainment and throw tons of money away for a hot dog. It's crazy. Even crazier is that we actually do sell ice cream here too, but thankfully few people seem to be interested this time of the year.

I've had a few training shifts so far and my parents actually don't seem to mind taking me there and picking me up. They said they'll sign me up for driving lessons soon, but I'm not so interested right now. I just want to go home. Like, *home* home.

I'm almost done my shift and I couldn't be happier. Mostly because it's so hectic working here. Between the stuck-up figure skaters and their tight little outfits, the horribly obnoxious hockey players, and the parents of all these kids, I feel like I've had enough. Not only do they treat me—and my coworkers—like the scum of the Earth, but I am also struggling a lot with giving back change. Every time I look for a one-dollar bill, my mind blanks out. The person at the counter usually either gives me a weird look or demands their change.

Loonies and toonies are not my friends. Neither are the people that frequent the rink. My coworkers are okay though, since they go through the same things I do. And Cherry's parents were actually super cool when I met them. But like, it's not cool to tell your friends that their parents are cool, so I didn't mention it to her.

I finish my shift just in time to scoot past the hungry hockey players who just finished their practice. They look about my age and I recognize some of them from my classes, but I kind of don't want them to see me so I duck my head and race to the front door. As soon as I go outside, I'm relieved at the thought of getting into a nice warm car.

Except there is no car. Actually, there are plenty of cars, but none of them are mine. I get my hopes up thinking that maybe Mom or Dad is behind another car, but as I skim past them, I realize they're not there at all. This is it. They've finally forgotten me. I should have known it would happen eventually.

With a sigh, I take out my cell and dial home with cold fingers. If they're home and seriously forgot about me, I'll be so mad. But it just keeps ringing. It almost goes to voicemail but then I hear someone pick up.

"Finally!" I say in my most annoyed voice. "I've been done work for like fifteen minutes. Where are you guys?"

There's a beat, and then… "Elli?"

"Who's that?" I say, just before it occurs to me. "Uncle Daniel? Do you know where Mom and Dad are?"

"Uhhh." That's not a good sound. "I think your dad's working late and your mom went grocery shopping or something."

Or something. "Well that's great," I say to him, just as I feel a few snowflakes land on my cheeks. "Yeah, can you just tell them that I died in a blizzard because they forgot about me?"

My uncle has the nerve to laugh out loud.

"Why is that funny?"

He stops laughing and says, "Sorry, kiddo. You just have a dry sense of humour, that's all."

"I was serious," I almost shout. I have to refrain from sounding stupid because some of the hockey players are coming out now.

He laughs again, but at least not as much as before. "I'm sorry about Rob and Shauna. But I'll come pick you up if you want."

I'm slightly ashamed that it never occurred to me that he might want to help out. Relieved, I say, "Yes please. That would be great."

"Where are you?" he asks.

"At the skating rink," I tell him. Someone whips past me and I almost fall over.

"I see you're fully immersing yourself in the culture," he says dryly as I glare at the person who was almost my demise.

"Yeah, yeah," I say, not bothering to even explain. I've lost my vocabulary because I realize I'm looking at Adrian. It was hard to tell at first because he's wearing a ridiculously large hat with flaps on the sides, but his gaze is unmistakable.

"Be there in two shakes," he says.

"Thanks," I mumble and the line goes dead.

I'm staring at Adrian who is staring at me with a half smile. When he realizes that I'm finished my conversation, his smile grows and he comes back toward me. What do I do, what do I do, what do I do?

"Hey," he says so smoothly I'm lost. "Sorry, I always seem to be knocking you over. Once you get into a hockey mindset, it's hard to get back out."

I have no idea what he means by that, but I manage to come up with the appropriate response to an apology. "That's okay."

He waves at a car behind him then turns his attention back to me. "We never really properly met. I'm Adrian."

He sticks out his hand and I shake it, because what else is there to do? There's a surprising amount of warmth emanating from his glove and it's all I can do to pull my bare hand away from it.

He lifts an eyebrow and says, "And you are…? Or should I just keep calling you Hawaii?"

Cute pet names aren't my thing, so that finally brings me back to myself. "I'm Elli."

A car horn honks and Adrian waves at his ride again, saying, "Yeah, yeah," even though they can't possibly hear him from here.

"Well, it's nice to finally meet you, Elli," he says. "I mean, after all those times I caught you staring at me, I figure I might as well have a name to put to those eyes."

My eyes narrow and I cock a hip with one hand on it. "Excuse me, but you're the one who's been staring at *me*."

"Hm, yeah, I guess you're right." He smiles again, all dimples, and I can't believe I'm having this conversation with him. I also can't believe he's coming on so strong or that I was able to have such a quick answer.

The car honks again and Adrian sighs audibly, for my benefit I'm sure. "Alright, I guess that's my final call. My brother's so impatient sometimes. Brothers, eh?"

I smile in what I hope is a cheeky way. "I wouldn't know, I don't have any."

"Must be nice," he says.

Then, he suddenly takes off his hat and *puts it on my head*. I try not to let it show that I'm freaking out, but I'm definitely freaking out. I know from movies that boys will offer sweaters to girls when they're cold, but that's not something that really happens back home.

"Stay warm, Hawaii," he says as he starts walking backwards away from me.

Finally he turns and I get a good look at his adorably messy hat head. I have no idea what just happened, but I pull the hat tighter onto my head, and press the fuzzy flaps against my cheeks. Maybe pet names aren't that bad.

My uncle arrives a few minutes later, and I gratefully climb into the car. It's hot inside, but I don't want to take the hat off yet.

"Nice hat," he says.

I shrug, not quite wanting to tell him where it's from. "Thank you so much for the ride."

Uncle Daniel nods and gives me a sideways glance. "Look, I wasn't going to say anything, but just as I was leaving your mom got home. I waited until she started carrying her groceries out to tell her I was picking you up. She looked like she felt bad and got into her car immediately and we basically raced to get here. I obviously won, but she's probably not happy about it. But don't say anything alright?"

"So, you don't really care about me, you're just competing with my mom?" I ask him.

He practically slams on the brakes at a stop sign. He's not usually a bad driver, so I must have caught him off guard. "That's not it at all, Elli. I wouldn't have come to get you if I didn't care. I was just telling you that your mom probably hates me even more now."

"Relax, Uncle Daniel, I was just kidding," I say to him, since it's mostly true anyway. "Dry humour, remember?" He just nods and I feel a little bad, like I've offended him. I twiddle my thumbs for a few seconds then ask, "So, why do you think Mom hates you?"

"Because she does," he answers simply.

"Why?" I'm not sure why I want to know so badly, but I do. I mean, he seems like an okay guy to me, and Mom doesn't usually have such strong feelings about other people.

He grunts, in a conceding sort of way. "I guess it might have something to do with showing up to their wedding slightly drunk." I barely have a chance to show my surprise, when he adds, "But I gave a fantastic speech, no one can deny that."

"How old were you?" I ask. It's probably rude to ask, but we're family so he'll just have to get over it.

"19," he says.

I do the math quickly and blurt out, "You can't possibly be 36."

I lean forward and study his face a little closer than I did before. Yes, I see some grey hairs and wrinkles at the corners of his eyes, but still. Wow. He could totally pass for a lot younger than that.

As we pull into the driveway, I ask before we can get out, "Was your speech really that great?"

He hesitates a moment before turning the ignition off. There are no cars in the driveway, which I guess means Mom really did go to find me at the rink. "No. It was terrible. I cried through half of it and confessed my love for Shauna right there in front of both our families."

My eyes widen. I can't imagine what a guy like Daniel would see in my mother, and I probably shouldn't even ask, but I say, "You didn't!"

He purses his lips and nods. "I know, hard to believe. But she was different back then. Thankfully, my brother got over it, but she never did. I think she's always thought I ruined her wedding or something."

"Do you still...?" I can't even finish my question, because I know I really shouldn't ask.

He frowns in such a deep and comical way that I have to laugh out loud, because the idea of him still liking my mom is way too creepy.

"Ugh, no," he says. "Happy for my brother, but I've had several successful relationships since then. I was just so young... Well, look who I'm talking to. You're young too, but you don't have a boyfriend. Do you?"

My mind briefly flits to Kai, but I don't think that counts. I shake my head.

"Good," he says as he finally opens his door. "Boys are trouble, Elli."

I think he's joking. But that still doesn't mean I'm going to tell him that the hat I'm wearing is from a really cute Canadian boy that I barely know, who has the most gorgeous eyes, and the most fun personality ever. That doesn't mean that I like Adrian, though, so don't get any ideas.

Mom pulls into the driveway just as we reach the front door. I'm afraid to see what will happen next as I hear her door slam shut, followed by the sound of her heeled boots clicking against the asphalt.

"Elli, I'm so sorry," she says as soon as she gets inside, sounding genuinely repentant.

"It's okay," I say sincerely. "Uncle Daniel came and got me."

Mom throws a glare his way, as if he's done something wrong, when really she's the one at fault. I feel bad for him, now that I know.

"Don't worry, Mom," I say, giving him a little smile. "We only hit two moose and three beavers along the way, but I'm still alive."

Daniel bursts out laughing, and I'm glad that I could diffuse that situation. Mom watches him walk away with a perplexed expression on her face.

I start up the staircase just as she asks, "Hey, where'd you get the hat?"

Ugh, what, is everyone going to mention the hat now? "Nowhere," I say cryptically as I continue to my room.

I check my email and find five emails from friends back home. None of them are from Kai, which disappoints me, but I'm happy to hear from my friends. Lily's got a new boyfriend named Devin, Sarah has to sit next to Anderson in math class (he's this super annoying preppy kid), Andrea got food poisoning from that sushi place we love but know we really should not go to. It's so much fun to hear about the antics they're up to, but it makes me miss them so much that it feels like someone punched me in the gut. Still, I get a little thrill when I tell them I'm coming for a visit as soon as I make the money. And then of course I have to tell them about my new job.

I consider emailing Kai, but my mom always says that I should let boys come to me. Ugh. So much waiting in my life.

CHAPTER EIGHT

Okay, I am really starting to get ticked off at school. I mean, school itself isn't that bad. People have actually started treating me like a normal person and having conversations with me. But I still always eat with Julian. Partially because I actually enjoy being with him, and also because I think I may be his only friend. I think Cherry would probably make a good friend for him too, but they never talk to each other and they barely acknowledge the other's existence. Which is a shame, because I'm really curious about what might have happened if they'd actually gone on their date.

Where was I going with this again?

Oh yeah. I'm getting really annoyed at school because there's this one big guy that likes to push Julian around. Actually, I've seen him do this to other people, too. And the worst part is that no one, especially not Jules, does anything about it! I'm pretty sure even a couple of teachers saw it happen once. (I can't say I'm blameless either, but the guy is at least six feet tall. I am 5'3", to put it into perspective.)

Today at lunch, I've finally decided to confront Jules about it.

"So, what's with the meathead?" I ask.

Julian's brow furrows above his glasses and he quickly glances at the jock table. "Which one?"

He probably thinks I'm referring to one of Adrian's friends. Yes, I told Jules about my little conversation with Adrian. I wouldn't have normally confided that kind of thing in a guy, but I didn't really know what the protocol with the whole hat thing was. Julian said that basically giving it back means I'm not interested in him and keeping it means that I'm definitely head over heels. No middle ground, whatsoever. I've been kind of on the fence about it, so I haven't given it back. But I don't wear it either. Not in public, anyway.

I drag my mind away from Adrian—who I haven't talked to in like a week, by the way—and back to the conversation at hand. "You know," I say, "the guy that thinks you're his punching bag."

"Not again, Elli, please," Jules says as he starts his usual habit of working on his homework. I can tell he's being extra serious because he called me "Elli" and not "Ella."

"No, seriously," I persist. "What is his deal? And why do you never stick up for yourself?" I feel a little guilty asking, because like I said, he's a pretty big guy, but I have to say something.

He sighs and peers at me over his glasses. "I have no idea what his *deal* is," he answers, making air quotes around the word "deal." "But I don't stick up for myself because Red is the top high school boxing champion in all of Ontario. So you see, Ella, it's much better to be pushed around every once in a while than to get into a fight with him."

He looks back down at his history textbook to let me know that the conversation is over for him. But it's not for me. I put my hands flat on the table and let out a frustrated breath.

"Well, that sucks," I say, even though I know Julian doesn't want to hear it. "You can't just be a bully for the sake of being a bully. The guy has no right!"

"Yeah, but he's got the muscles for it," Jules says wearily. "You're right though, he has a very strong sense of entitlement, and even the teachers give in to it."

"Hmph." I lean back again and cross my arms. "Next time I see Red, I'm going to give him a piece of my mind."

"*Ella.*"

"What?"

Jules shakes his head. "I've never seen him hit a girl, but I wouldn't put it past him. Just leave it be and let me take it."

A flicker of admiration wells up inside of me at Julian's toughness, regardless of the fact that I don't agree with his philanthropic approach to the situation. I mean, there's got to be something that can be done, right? I decide to leave it alone like Julian asked, but I do put it aside to think about later.

*　　*　　*

I got invited to a party tonight. I don't really know Andy, the girl who invited me that well, but she was really nice. My parents are at some charity event, so I decide to go. Back home, I used to go to like every party ever, even ones that I wasn't explicitly invited to. It almost felt like being my normal self to go out.

But now that I'm here, I feel like a wallflower. I don't know anyone, so I'm kind of sticking by the drinks table, nodding my head to the music. Before I got here, I felt a little guilty for not inviting Julian. Now I really regret not having dragged him with me because I'm feeling rather lonely.

I feel really out of place, so I decide to leave way earlier than is socially acceptable. I say goodbye to Andy and call a taxi to pick me up. Someone tugs on my arm as I'm heading to the front door and I turn to see Adrian.

"Hey," he says with a huge smile.

"Hi, Adrian," I say, genuinely happy to see him. I almost wish I hadn't called the taxi yet.

"I didn't know you'd be here," he says. "Come on, we should go dance." He nods his head in the direction of the makeshift dance floor in the middle of the living room.

"Oh…" I say. "Well, I was actually just leaving. Sorry."

He frowns in disappointment. "All right…"

"Next time?" I offer.

"I'll take you up on that." He gives me a beautiful smile before heading over to hang out with his friends.

I watch him a moment longer, shake my head, then continue on my way. I reach the front door just as I get a text telling me that my taxi is here. Just as I open the door, in steps Red, Ontario high school boxing champ.

I look up straight into his dark hazel eyes. Recognition flashes in them and I wonder if I should say something. Then he nods at me, looks away, and smiles in someone else's direction. (I refuse to acknowledge that it's a kind of a nice smile.) I follow his movement and watch him almost bowl over three people to get to a girl in the middle of a crowded living room. She smiles sweetly, which makes me want to hurl.

Maybe I'm wrong. Maybe he just doesn't know his own strength, maybe he's not totally aware of his surroundings, so when he tries to get somewhere he just kind of accidentally knocks into people. Maybe he's not so bad.

People kind of respectfully—or maybe fearfully—keep their distance except one guy. This guy either didn't see the interaction between Red and the girl, or doesn't care because he's standing far too close to Red's girl. The next thing I know, Red is very purposefully shoving him to the edge of the dance floor, where he trips, knocks some other girl's punch all over her dress, and stumbles away in embarrassment.

Yeah, pretty sure I had this guy pegged from the start.

*   *   *

Now I'm chilling alone in my room, doing my homework instead of dancing with Adrian because I couldn't just make up my mind. My uncle has unsurprisingly gone to whatever hole where he spends all his time. I like my uncle, but I actually don't know that much about him, like what he does with himself, where he works…that kind of thing.

CRASH!

I jolt off of my bed at the sound downstairs. I hear some clattering around, and I'm scared out of my mind. I wonder if I should call the police, but the noises have stopped. Maybe I'll just check it out first. Just in case, I pick up the heaviest thing in my room—it's a dictionary. Who knows, maybe we're being robbed by an illiterate.

When I go downstairs and peer around the corner of the wall that separates the front entrance from the living room, a wave of relief washes over me. Uncle Daniel is here. I guess he knocked over the coffee table and he's trying to set it right. Something about him is off.

"Uncle Daniel, you scared the crap outta me," I tell him. I don't mean to be harsh, but I am seriously grateful I'm not here with a murderer or something.

He turns to me with half-lidded eyes. "Elli," he slurs, "go back upstairs."

It dawns on me that he's drunk. I guess I shouldn't be surprised after the story he told me, but I am. Instead of listening to him, I come a little closer.

"Please," he says, sounding oddly desperate. "I don't want you to see me like this."

"How much did you drink?" I ask him, proud of myself for sounding more concerned than disappointed, even though I feel the opposite.

He runs a hand over his head and laughs a little. "I always knew you were too smart to be part of this family."

Whatever that means. He teeters a little and I rush over to help him down to the couch. He's not a big guy, but I guess when you're drunk, you have no idea where you're putting your weight. We sit down awkwardly on the couch. I get up almost immediately and he starts to fall over. I see I'm going to have to do something about him.

"Here," I say loudly to make sure he's listening as I stuff a pillow behind his head. "I'm going to get you some water and chips, okay? Just sit tight."

"Sure, but you don't have to yell, Elli," he says, looking disgruntled.

Whoops. Oh well, he'll just have to deal with it, since I'm doing him a huge favour at the moment. I pour some cold filtered water in a glass and grab a bag of salt and vinegar chips, then bring them back to the living room. I can't tell if my uncle's asleep or not, since his eyes are closed, but I take the chance on waking him because I'm actually kind of worried about him now.

"Uncle Daniel," I say, shaking him until he rouses.

"Oh, thank God," he says when he sees the chips. "I'm so hungry."

"No, drink this first." I hand him the water and pull the chips out of his reach.

He grunts and offers me a scowl, but takes a big gulp of the water. "You're so bossy," he says in a whiny voice.

"And you're drunk," I remind him.

"Good point." He groans a little and reaches for the chips that I finally give him. He curses and I look away because now I know why he said he didn't want me to see him like this. "Your parents are going to kick me out when they find me drunk. I'm such a mess."

"Then you should probably drink more water and go have a hot shower," I tell him. And I mean it. I don't know what his life is like, but I get the impression that he needs to stay here for a while.

"You're so nice to me, Elli," he says. "You're like, the nicest person to me. I know all drunk people say that, but it's really true. You're nice."

Gee, thanks. "Yeah, umm…thanks. So, what's going on? I'm not going to have to deal with any of your friends showing up, am I?" I don't know why I thought that, but I figured it'd be good to ask.

"As if I have any friends," Daniel mumbles. "You know, I used to be really cool. I was so cool."

"Yeah?" I say, forcing the water back into his hand in an attempt to bring him back to soberdom.

"Yeah. In high school, I was a champion, you know?" he sounds less slurry now, but he's still sputtering what sounds like nonsense. "I was like Muhammad Ali. Float like a…float like a bee. No, what is it?"

"Float like a butterfly, sting like a bee?" I hope that's the one he's looking for, because I don't quite feel like searching for similes right now.

"That's the one. I floated and I stung." He closes his eyes. I don't want to lose him.

"What are you talking about?" I ask, jiggling his shoulder a little.

His eyes flutter open. He puts his fists up in front of his face and though he's a little unsteady, it looks as though he's familiar with the stance. "Boxing. I wasn't top of my class in academics, but I was a great boxer. The greatest."

I frown in thought. "What, at my school?"

He exaggerates a nod. "Yup. That's the one."

What is it with boxing at that school? I don't ask. Instead, I say, "So what, do you still box now?"

He laughs bitterly, but I can tell the water and chips are starting to help him be a little clearer. "Not a chance. Everything went downhill from there."

"Really?" I ask sympathetically, actually meaning it. "What happened?"

"Drugs," he answers. "Sex, alcohol. I really shouldn't be talking to you about this."

I try not to show my shock or confusion. I'm missing pieces of the story, pieces I'll probably always miss. I'm starting to wonder if Daniel was dealt a bad hand in life, or if he chose it for himself. I shouldn't ask, I shouldn't ask, I know I should definitely not ask.

"Nothing really works out for you, does it?" I ask him anyway.

He looks into my eyes, a mixture of sadness and guilt hidden there. "Not really. But that's probably mostly my fault."

I'm not sure what to do or say. I'm not sure what level of comfort is appropriate to give, considering the circumstances. So I go for something neutral, but still helpful.

"Look, Uncle Daniel," I say to him, "Mom and Dad are going to be home soon. Why don't you go take a quick shower and then we can maybe finish off this bag? You'll feel much better in no time."

Physically. Mentally, I'm not sure any amount of showering can help.

"You really are a great kid, Elli," he says with a small smile.

When Mom and Dad do get home later that night, I know they're surprised to find me and Uncle Daniel playing a car racing game. Daniel still has a bit of a buzz, but his depression took a turn for the better when I suggested hanging out with a video game and now he seems okay.

"I cannot believe how good you are at drifting!" Uncle Daniel exclaims just as my parents walk in.

I laugh and wave very quickly at them before turning back to the game. I'm not supposed to "let" my uncle win any games, but I suspect that he's been doing that for me.

"Elli, it's past your bedtime," Mom says stiffly.

I frown, because I don't have a bedtime, but I don't get a chance to say anything before dad says, "It's Saturday. Let her live a little."

My dad is my hero. My mom needs to get over the past or whatever is bugging her. Mom narrows her eyes at Daniel who smiles kindly at her. It's the perfect opportunity to side-swipe his car and take the lead.

"Aw, not again," he says in a mock-angry tone.

When the race finishes, I say, "I probably should go to bed. I can't believe how late it got."

My parents are gone, but he says in a low voice, "Listen, about earlier…"

"I know," I say. "I won't say anything about it, but you have to promise me something."

"What?" he asks uncertainly.

"Promise you'll lay off the drinking," I say, gauging his reaction. "Like, a lot."

He looks guilty, which makes me feel bad. However, I don't want to back down on this point. With a tight smile, he nods. He may or may not mean it, but what he doesn't know is that I'm going to be checking in on him. Whether he likes it or not. Because if you ask me, Daniel deserves more out of this life than what he's giving himself.

"Alright, Elli, you got me," he concedes.

"Goodnight, Uncle Daniel."

"Can you just call me Dan or something?" he says suddenly. "You make me feel old with all that uncle stuff."

I laugh. "Sure, Dan."

CHAPTER NINE

I'm hanging out with Cherry on my break. I see her every once in a while at the rink. I'm not sure if she has real reasons for being here, or if she comes just because I'm here, but I kind of like it. I actually once caught Cherry out on the ice during a public skate and she looked...well, she looked really graceful and surprisingly athletic. I never would have guessed, but now I can't unsee the image of her practically floating across the smooth surface, her hands out and behind her as if she were some sort of a bird in the sky.

I know I just compared Cherry to a bird, but it was really magical, okay? There, I said it. And now I'm starting to wish I could float on ice, but the very thought terrifies me. As it is, I'm watching a bunch of teenage boys flail across the ice in heavy equipment, slashing sticks around in hopes of hitting a tiny little black thing. I do not get hockey.

"Yo, Ella." Cherry's snapping her fingers in my face. "Wow, you zone out so easily. So, how about it?"

"How about what?" I ask, feeling guilty that I've missed part of what she said. I'd been having a hard time keeping track of where Adrian was until Cherry informed me that he's number 46. It made it a little easier, but these guys move fast.

She laughs and kind of sighs a little. "You missed everything, didn't you? Okay, I was trying to tell you how after the hockey practice, we clear off the ice with the Zamboni and well...technically public skating starts an hour after hockey, but we could go on before then. It's so great when the ice is all fresh and smooth. So?"

"Me? Out there?" I gesture loosely in the direction of the rink. Has Cherry been reading my mind or something? Except, no, I can't do that. I'll die. "Umm...well, I don't own skates, so I guess not."

Cherry gives me this incredulous look and I know there's no way out. "We have skates here. Come on, Ella, it'll be fun!"

I hesitate, even though the offer is really good. "I don't...I can't skate."

"I know. I want to teach you!" She's so enthusiastic about it that I can't see how I can say no. "Plus, the best part is that I'll be the only one to see you fall. On your butt. Which will happen. But," she looks behind me for a second, "you got a little bit of padding back there, so it shouldn't be too bad."

My face goes red, and I can't help but mentally compare my physique to Cherry's. I'm a tiny little girl who's still waiting for the appropriate amount of curves. But Cherry... She's certainly not overweight, but man does she have all the right curves in all the right places. I'm not jealous, but I probably could be if she dressed differently.

Finally, I give in. "I'll have to call my parents to let them knowing I'm staying late, but—"

"Yes!" she practically shouts and a wide grin appears on her bright red lips. "I just know you'll make an excellent skater."

"We'll see about that, Cherry," I say with a shy smile. She's been so nice to me that I can't really deny her. Plus, who knows, maybe I *could* make a great skater?

A couple of hours later, as I hobble to the ice in what feels like the tightest pair of shoes ever, I begin to rethink this plan. "Maybe this wasn't such a good idea," I say to Cherry as I clutch her hand.

"I know, the rubber floor makes it seem really awkward," she explains. "But it's totally different on the ice, you'll see."

Oh, yes—it's different all right. Not easier, but definitely different. I should really start paying better attention to the wording people use.

Cherry starts off by pulling me behind her while she effortlessly swishes her legs back and forth. I'm terrified by the sensation of it and my legs lock in place, which according to her, makes things worse. So, now she's trying a variety of techniques to get me to move including skating backwards while holding onto both my hands, pushing me from behind, and even crouching down and individually moving each of my legs. None of it is working because if I move, I will fall and die.

Which Cherry thinks is funny, judging by how she's laughing. "Ella, come on. Haven't you ever been rollerblading before? It's the same thing."

"No," I admit. "Some of my friends do it, but I always biked everywhere."

"Well, we'll just have to take this one step at a time," she says. "Literally, like take a step. But don't pick up your feet. Just push off one foot and let the other one follow."

I take a deep breath and out of the corner of my eye, I'm aware of someone in the stands watching us. I figure it's a janitor or something, so I do exactly what Cherry says. Push off, let follow. I did it! I'm so proud of myself that I hear clapping, and realize it's Cherry, and she's even cheering for me.

I do it a couple more times, alternating my feet, and I'm so happy and free and moving way too fast. And then I fall flat on my butt, like Cherry predicted. I'm surprised it doesn't hurt that much.

Cherry gasps and I think I've done something horribly wrong until she says, "That was perfect!"

"I fell," I say with a groan.

"I know, but you fell so wonderfully," she says like she really, actually means it. Thankfully, she reaches down and helps me up. I have no idea how I would've gotten up without her.

"Thanks," I say, trying to brush ice dust off my backside. I look around and see that whoever was watching us before is gone, and I feel better about my little tumble.

"You had a good rhythm going," she says, looking happy. Happy for me, because I'm doing something she likes. That's kind of sweet. "Here, take my hand again and I'll help you even it out."

I muster up my courage and take Cherry's hand again. She insisted I wear thin gloves and I'm glad for them now. Because when I fell I hit my hands hard, and I imagine it would have been worse without the gloves. Cherry starts going slowly and I try to mimic her movements. She doesn't seem to mind that I'm crushing her hand, which leads me to believe that she is probably the nicest person I know.

When I feel like everything is finally under control, I decide to start up a conversation. "So," *swish*, "what's going on between you and Julian?"

Cherry falters for half a second but not enough to knock us off balance.

Swish.

Swish.

Swish.

"Cherry, did you hear me?" I ask softly, hoping I didn't offend her or something.

"Yeah, I'm just not sure how to answer you," she says. She sounds shy, like I've asked her who her celebrity crush is.

"Start from the beginning," I suggest gently.

Cherry whirls around so that she's skating backwards and facing me, but she doesn't let go of my hand. "Jules and I didn't know each other that well. We're both kind of loners, in case you haven't noticed." She gives me a wry smile. "But when a guy starts looking at you a certain way, you start to see him a certain way."

Now Cherry lets go of my hand which scares me until I realize I'm steady on my own. She swirls around a couple of times and I'm so mesmerized, I almost forget to keep pushing off.

"We started talking a little bit, and I thought he was kinda cool." There's a wistfulness to her voice while she tells the story. "So, I asked him out. He seemed pretty happy about it, but then he never showed. End of story."

She skates away abruptly to do some fancy footwork and more turns, while I'm left with my thoughts. She told me basically the same story I got from Julian, but he never told me she was the one who asked him out.

"You don't look surprised," she says as she comes back to me.

"I'm sorry," I say, and I'm sure I have a guilty look on my face. "He kind of told me about that."

"Oh," she says slowly. I feel so bad. "Well, did he tell you why? Because I'd really like to know why."

I shake my head, my eyebrows all scrunched up together. "You never asked him?"

Cherry purses her lips to the side like she has something to say but doesn't want to say it. "I think he tried to tell me once, but I was too angry at the time to listen. We haven't spoken since." She shrugs.

There has got to be a really good reason why Julian stood Cherry up. Anyone with eyes can see that she's amazing, especially him. I narrow my eyes and think of the most devious ways of getting him to spill his guts to me. I have a job, a purpose now before I go back to my home permanently.

Obviously, I'll have to take it upon myself to right some wrongs here.

"Ugh, of all the guys at our school," she says, "and Julian turned out to be a heartbreaker. Typical."

But he's not typical. I know he's not. And I'm going to find a way to fix it.

*   *   *

The next day at school, I have a little spring in my step. I have a mission now. I'm going to make Julian spill his guts to me, and then I'm going to make him make it up to Cherry. How I'll accomplish this, I have no idea. But I will.

I pass by the announcements board, where the big ad for the boxing tournament is still front and centre. Now that I know about Red, I wonder why anyone would willingly choose to join the boxing team. I mean, aren't they afraid to get completely pummelled by him?

It makes me think about Unc—Dan. We haven't really talked much since that night that he came home drunk, but I've been secretly keeping tabs on him. He totally does not seem like the boxing type, but maybe that's because I really only have a few examples to go on. Aggressive, fit, agile—not exactly traits that I would attribute to Dan.

At lunch, I am positively bursting with energy and I know Julian can tell. He gives me this look like he's afraid of what I can do in this state of mind, and maybe he should be afraid.

I'm trying to come up with a tactful way of bringing up Cherry when Julian says, "You know, I never really asked you about Hawaii. It seems like a neat place."

"Neat?" I spit the word out. "It's not neat, it's amazing! I mean, there's a reason they call it Paradise. Everything there is perfect."

"Sorry you have to be here, then," he mumbles.

I look at his pale face that has lost any sort of emotion and gulp down my stupid words. "I didn't really mean it that way. Sorry. Um, can we just go back and you ask me again?"

Jules gives me that over-the-glasses look that he loves so much, but he obliges anyway. "What's Hawaii like?"

I smile. "It's amazing. You'd really like it. No snow, so that's kinda crappy, but it has its moments."

He smiles back at me and his perfectly straight teeth gleam. "That is kinda crappy. I can't imagine why anyone would ever want to live in a place where it's always hot."

"I know, right?" I tease back. I pause a moment and think. Maybe if I open up to Jules, he'll open up to me. "I'm still sore over the move because, well I mean, that's my home and all my friends were there. But I also almost had a boyfriend. And he kinda stopped messaging me, so I can only assume he's forgotten about me."

Although that was really hard for me to say, it's all true. Kai did stop messaging me, which makes me really sad. But on the other hand, who could blame him? I'm over here and he's over there.

Jules gives me a sympathetic look and says, "I imagine you're very difficult to forget, so either he's an idiot or something else is going on."

I can't help but smile and blush a little bit. "That's really sweet of you to say."

He shrugs and looks down at his hands. I've embarrassed him. Not good. Think of something else to say, Elli.

"Speaking of boyfriends," I start, having absolutely no idea where I'm going with that, "have you ever been one?"

Julian raises one coy eyebrow at me and doesn't even deign to answer my question. "So like, do people go to school in bikinis in Hawaii?" he asks.

"Yeah, 'cause we have school on the beach, and that's totally school appropriate," I deadpan. "Speaking of bikinis...you ever seen Cherry in one?"

Julian's eyes widen. Oops, a little too strong. "Seriously, Elli. When I said I didn't want to talk about it, I really meant that I didn't want to talk about it."

"Ugh." I slouch down in my seat. "The amount of things you and Cherry don't want to talk about is equivalent to the things you do talk about."

"You've been talking to Cherry about me?" he asks. To his credit, he sounds more curious than upset.

"I'd say it's more the other way around," I tell him cryptically.

It worked. He's hooked. "What did she say, exactly?"

"Wouldn't you like to know?"

"Well, I would," he says smugly. "But the bell's about to ring."

And then it does, and for one second I believe he's psychic or something. But he's not; he just knows this school very well. I roll my eyes as I follow him out of the caf. I almost got somewhere. This sucks.

"Cheer up, Ella," he says in a teasing voice. "There are plenty of potential almost boyfriends here in Canada for you."

I laugh at Julian's stupid joke because really, what does one say to that? My laughter is abruptly cut off when Julian is propelled forward and lands on the ground in front of us. I swivel my head around to see what happened, though it should be obvious the way the other students are parting like the Red Sea.

Red.

It's him.

I'm livid. I stomp right up to him, despite Julian's protests, and cut Red off in his tracks. With my arms crossed and my face displaying what I hope is an intimidating scowl, I say to him, "Hey! You can't just push people over whenever you feel like it!"

I can feel the other students' stares as they wait for Red's reaction. He doesn't say anything. Instead, he puts out one hand and pushes me to the side. Perhaps he didn't mean to knock me over, but he caught me off guard and I barely have time to put my hands out and catch myself before I hit the floor.

I can't believe it. Julian was right.

CHAPTER TEN

Julian recovers quickly and suddenly he's racing after Red. He glances at me briefly, but I tell him I'm okay and he just keeps going until he's caught up to the meathead. Julian does exactly what I did which was to stand straight in Red's path. I'm terrified for his safety and wish I'd never stepped in. I'm already back on my feet when Jules starts his tirade.

"Oh, you think you're so tough because you can take out some tiny little girl and a nerdy kid?" he says defiantly.

I'm not a tiny little girl... Okay, everyone is tiny compared to Red. Except Jules. I never quite realized how tall Julian is, since we're always sitting together, but he's actually taller than Red.

"What are you gonna do about it?" Red growls.

So it speaks.

I stand next to Julian and say, "You don't want to mess with this kid."

I'm talking to Red, not Julian. Red doesn't exactly look like the intellectual type, so I'm hoping that maybe I can bluff my way out of this. "He—he has anger issues. He'll just go off on you and it won't be good."

I can feel the confusion radiating off of Julian, but he doesn't disagree. Maybe he'll work with me on this.

"Is that so?" Red says with a little smirk. Uh oh. Maybe he has more brain cells than I originally thought. "Let's see what you got then." He puts up his fists and I just about faint.

"Not here!" Julian says frantically.

I can tell the other students are trying to decide whether they should stay to catch the fight or hurry to their classes before they're late.

"Yeah, not here," I agree. "You'll get suspended."

Red snorts and throws a lazy punch past Jules' face that I realize was just his warm-up. *Think, Elli, think.*

"No!" I say so forcefully Red drops his hands in shock. "He'll take you on in that stupid boxing tournament. Then you'll see what I really meant."

Don't back down, Julian, please don't back down. Most of the other students have realized that nothing interesting is going to happen here, so they've left.

"Hm," Red muses, like he is actually capable of musing. "Fine. See you there, loser."

"Yeah, you'll see me there!" Julian calls to Red's retreating back. Everyone else rushes away to make their classes, but we stay behind.

"What the heck, Elli?" Jules says once the crowd has dispersed. He's covering his face with his hands, as if shutting his eyes could take back everything we just said and did.

"It's fine, Jules," I say with a shaky voice. "Really. Let's just go to math."

"Let's just go to math?" he repeats incredulously, finally showing his face. It's red and his eyes look like they'll bulge out of their sockets. I've never seen him so...so not placid. It's a good look for him.

"Do you have any idea when that tournament is, Elli?" he asks.

We're totally late for math now, but at this point I guess it'd be better just to skip and deal with the monster we've created. I take him by the arm

74

and lead him away from the empty hallway as we continue our conversation.

"No?" I say. I feel bad. I really do.

"It's in three months!" he exclaims.

"Great," I say cheerfully. I receive a glare that I most definitely deserve, but I'm not ready to desert him just yet.

"Not great," he says. "Terrible."

I pull harder on his arm and take him back to the cafeteria where some students are spending their free periods. I can't have him making such a huge scene in the hall where a teacher could find us.

"Are you listening to me, Elli?" he asks, his voice stern in a way that I guess I'm supposed to take to mean that he's mad at me.

"Look, I take full responsibility for my actions just now, but you didn't exactly back down, or just take the hit and walk away," I tell him. He looks like he wants to retort but he knows I'm telling the truth. "And I'm proud of you. I'll help you figure this thing out, alright?"

He swallows a few big gulps of air and takes a seat in the closest available chair. Dumping his backpack on the floor, he asks, "Help me figure what out?"

"How we're going to get you into the tournament," I say. Isn't that what this is all about?

"You think I'm actually going to fight that guy?" he says, raising his voice again. "Are you insane? I'll be killed."

"Shhh, relax," I say, looking around nervously. No one needs to hear us right now. "You will not be killed. Half that guy's fight is in his bravado. Which you just proved you could match."

Julian's face flushes and he almost smiles. "I kinda did, didn't I?"

"And you kinda liked it," I say, this time coaxing a full smile out of him.

"I have to admit, it was invigorating." His face sobers again. "But I still can't fight him, Ella. I mean, look at me."

I do look at him. He's not skinny, which is actually to his advantage. But he'd have to start working out and training right away. I have to wonder if this is doable. I look back up into Julian's gaze. There's a fire in his eyes now that's undeniable, and suddenly I feel like that's all he might need.

"Imagine, Julian," I say wistfully, "you could be the one to put Red in his place."

"I—I…" he's going to say that he can't, that he's not cut out for that kind of thing, that he shouldn't do it. Except he doesn't say that. "I don't even know where to start."

My heart lifts for a moment and I can't help but throw my arms around him. He did, after all, stand up for me and me alone, when he wouldn't even do that for himself. I figure I owe him.

"First, we need to sign you up for the tournament," I say, grabbing his arm once again. I start pulling him in the direction of the guidance office and he doesn't even complain as he hastily grabs his backpack. "Second, we need to get you an instructor. And third, you have to start working out and training like…today."

"There are so many problems with this," he says, his voice wavering. "I mean, where am I supposed to get a boxing instructor this late? And also, me and physical activity? Not a good combination."

"Oh, you can do anything you set your mind to, Jules," I tell him just as we reach the office. "And I think I know someone who can help us."

I haven't even stopped to think about what I'm doing. I can't think about the implications of putting my friend in such a predicament. I just hope my uncle won't wig out on me when I ask him to teach my friend to box in just three months.

This can be done. I'll do everything it takes to make Julian into a hero, because I honestly believe he has a hero's heart.

"Hi, Ms. Robertson," I say brightly as soon as I walk into the office. The receptionist has her head bent over her work, but as soon as she looks up and sees me, she smiles. Yes, another friend. That's always good to have.

"What can I do for you, deary?" she asks pleasantly.

Julian frowns at our seeming familiarity. I say, "We're just wondering how we can sign up for the boxing tournament."

"That's not exactly the type of sport I'd expect you to be interested in," she says patronizingly.

I try not to groan at her fifties-esque way of thinking and instead force my smile to stay in place. "It's for Julian." I point to him. Then I have an idea. "But actually, do you have a ladies' boxing tourney? I wouldn't mind trying that."

Ms. Robertson looks sceptically at both of us. "Well, you don't look like the type either," she says, looking pointedly at Julian. "But to each his own. All you need to do is fill out the proper forms. Let me just find them."

As she scuttles to the back of her office, Julian whispers, "Elli, what are you doing? It's not like they'll let you fight Red, too."

Oh, how I'd love to. "No, but I can train with you," I tell him. "It'll be a little bonding exercise."

He huffs, but I can tell that he's actually pleasantly surprised at my support. Again, it's the least I can do since I basically got him into this mess. I squeeze his arm to show that I really mean it. He awkwardly pats my hand, which I'm sure means that he appreciates me a lot and I'm his best friend.

Only once we've filled out the forms and handed them back to Ms. Robertson have I finally been able to slow down and really think. And what I think is that I have no idea what I'm doing. I've just signed me and Julian up for a boxing tournament regardless of the fact that neither of us knows anything about boxing. Not only that, but we don't really have an instructor and I'm not even sure I can get one.

Plus, I have to agree with Julian when he says that he doesn't do physical activity, because I don't either. I mean, yeah I used to go swimming back home all the time, but that was more for the boys than anything else. Ugh, what was I thinking?

"Elli, I sincerely hope you actually know someone who can help us. Or else, I hope you're okay with me switching schools and never fighting your battles again." I wish Julian were joking, but a part of me knows that he's not.

We're wandering aimlessly around the school now, since the period isn't over yet. I shrug. "My uncle was the boxing champion at this school. We're on good terms, so I don't see why he wouldn't help."

"Why do you not sound confident in that belief?" he asks me.

"I don't know." I decide to go for full honesty. "It was kind of the highlight of his life, but I get the feeling that he'd rather leave it in the past. Still, we can ask him."

"Right," Julian says. He's still not convinced. "And how long ago was this?"

"Oh, I don't know…eighteen years or so?" I answer.

Julian groans. "I had no idea you were this impulsive."

I need to interject here and say that I am not impulsive and never have been. The craziest thing I've ever done is kiss a boy before leaving the country. Oh, and one time I did a cliff dive, but that was for a dare, and it was very carefully planned out.

But I don't tell Julian that. Instead, I say, "See? We're already getting to know each other better. I had no idea you were capable of getting so angry."

"I'm not angry," he mutters.

"But you were," I remind him. He doesn't answer, so I change the subject. "If you come home with me after school, we can talk to my uncle right away."

"Might as well," he mumbles. "Since I have to get started today, as you say."

He's not happy. And why should he be? His life has just been totally turned upside down and he knows exactly what he's in for, and he doesn't like it or want it. I want to make that better for him, but I'm not sure how I can.

"I'm sorry," I say after several minutes. "I should have just left it alone like you told me."

He shakes his head and looks down at me, his gaze softening a bit. "I'm sorry, too," he says. "For not being able to just take him out right on the spot."

I smile. "You'll have your chance."

*   *   *

Later on, I'm surprised to see my uncle has come to the school to pick me up. I never asked him to and I can't imagine my parents asking him to do that. He must have come of his own volition. What luck I'm having today.

"Hey, kid," he says out the passenger side window. "Get in."

"Hi, Unc—Dan. Hi, Dan," I say as I open the door. "My friend Julian is coming over to do some homework." I can make that the truth later.

Dan takes a quick peek at Julian and motions him into the backseat. "That's almost believable," he says under his breath.

"Dan, come on," I whisper back, even as I feel myself blushing.

Dan laughs. "Sorry. And you are?" he asks Julian through the rearview mirror.

"Julian," he answers. "Or just Jules, most people call me."

"How come you came today?" I ask Dan.

He shrugs. "I know you hate the cold. Truth is, though, you're starting to grow on me. I think you're a good influence."

I laugh because everything my uncle says to me is funny. I love it. "Isn't it supposed to be the other way?"

"Not when you're so much more grown up than I am," he answers. And of course, the grilling starts. "So, are you Elli's boyfriend? Because she told me she didn't have one."

"I'm not," Julian answers at the same time I say, "He's not."

"Actually," Julian continues. Actually what? "I'm pretty sure she's crushing on someone else, so that takes care of that."

I nearly choke.

"Well, that's news to me," Uncle Dan says. "Were you just lying to me or something, Elli?"

"Of course not," I answer him. I think. "Julian just has a very strong imagination."

In the backseat I hear Julian scoff at me.

"Look, Uncle Dan," I start slowly, "the real reason I'm bringing Julian home with me is because we wanted to talk to you."

Dan is silent for a moment, then he says in a confused voice, "About...?"

I look at Julian for a second and he nods, which is all the encouragement I need. "We want you to teach us to box. Or more specifically, Julian needs to learn to do it."

Dan doesn't say anything. Not a single word. But his driving is getting that edge again. I know what that means. Finally, when I think I've broken his brain, he screeches to a halt at the side of the road by our house.

"Um, that's a no in case you couldn't guess," he says. Then he gets out of his car, slams the door shut, and stalks to the house.

"So…is this why you got the feeling he'd rather not bring up his golden years?" Julian asks. He sounds a little angry, but I haven't given up yet.

"Come on," I say, leading him into my house. "Dan!" I call. "Where are you?"

"In the kitchen, ignoring you," he answers. At least he's sort of back to joking.

I find him in the kitchen, rummaging around in the fridge. "Was that a final no, or will this just take a little convincing?"

"Yeah, my answer's final, Regis," he says, not bothering to look up at me.

Julian is standing awkwardly behind me, like he's not sure what to do with himself. I am also not sure what to do with myself. Finally, Dan stretches back up with food stuffed into his hands.

"Uh, don't you guys have homework to do?" he says dismissively. He sits down at the table and starts fixing what looks like the grossest ham and herring sandwich ever. "Or whatever that's a euphemism for."

Okay, now I'm starting to get fed up. "But Dan—"

"No's a no, Elli," Dan says.

"Excuse me," Julian says as he moves me gently out of the way and goes to sit across from Dan at the table. "Look, man, I know you don't know me from a hole in the ground, but I could really, really use your help. See, I just signed up for the boxing tournament at school which is in like three months, and believe me—I'm surprised I'm doing it, too. But I need to do this, so is there any way I can get you to agree?"

"No," Dan says before shoving a huge bite of his sandwich into his mouth. Julian just stares at him until he swallows down his food. "Why do you think this is my problem, anyway?"

Julian glances at me, gives me a kind of half smile, then looks back at Dan. "Today, Elli got shoved by this guy that normally just picks on me. She was standing up for me, and he didn't like it. I called him out on it and somehow ended up agreeing to go up against him in the boxing tournament. He's won the tournament three years in a row, and I haven't done anything in sports since track and field in grade six."

Dan has stopped eating and is staring at me like I have two heads. It's disconcerting, but then I see his expression start to change to something new that I don't recognize.

"And why do *you* need to learn to box?" he asks me.

"Because I promised I'd help Julian in any way I can," I answer. "I did sort of get him into this mess."

"You guys are doing this just to take down some stupid bully?" he asks. I can't tell if he believes us or not, so I nod vigorously. "Why didn't you just say so in the first place?"

"You'll do it?" I squeal.

"I guess so," he answers. I rush over to him and hug him so hard he has to push me away a little. "But it won't be easy, especially since no one in this room is in any shape whatsoever."

I look over at Julian and he actually looks sort of okay. He smiles at me and at Uncle Dan, then he claps his hands together.

"Let's do it," Julian says.

CHAPTER ELEVEN

I'm starting to doubt what my uncle said about being a great boxer. I mean, he was drunk after all, and I just totally fell for it. Yesterday, when Julian and I told Dan we wanted to start right away, he was suspiciously compliant. And then we...didn't really do anything. Well no, that's not true. We worked on our "stances" for two hours.

Jules—who is giving me the silent treatment right now, but still eating lunch with me—was ready to give up about eleven times. On the twelfth time, Dan slapped him—yes, literally—and told him to "grow a pair." His words, not mine. After that, Jules stopped complaining, but he's certainly not happy.

"Jules?" I say timidly.

"Mmhmm."

I know how interesting a social science textbook can be, but this is ridiculous. He won't even look at me, so why is he bothering to sit with me?

"I'm sorry," I say.

He shrugs and asks, "For what?" He's still not looking at me.

"For my uncle," I answer. Okay, it's not the whole truth. "And for the whole boxing and Red thing. And..." I've lost him. "And I'm sorry you think social science is so cool."

Finally he looks up at me with a confused look. "What?"

I smile now that he's looking at me. "I really am sorry, okay? I should have just kept my mouth shut."

Julian's shoulders lose their tension and his expression softens. "It's all right, Ella. You said it yourself, I didn't back down and I could have. It's time I faced him."

"That's really cool," I tell him.

"Yeah," he says. "Like social science."

He smiles at me which allows me to laugh at his joke. Maybe he's not as angry as I thought he was.

*   *   *

Amazingly, Dan keeps his word to keep training me and Jules. We work with him whenever we're not at school or work and he's available. Which seems to be all the time. In fact, I'm starting to wonder what Dan did with his time before we enlisted his help. It seems like every time I call or text him to say that Julian and I have free time, he's already at home waiting for us.

It's been a week since we started training. I told my parents about it yesterday, because it was getting too hard to come up with excuses as to why we rearranged the basement, why Jules comes over all the time, and why we hang out with my uncle in the basement. I thought my explanation would put their dear little hearts at ease, but it didn't.

At first they didn't believe us, but Dad had no choice but to believe his own brother. He knows all about Dan's glory days and eventual decline. After that, Mom got mad at Dan for "being a bad influence" and making me try boxing, and Dad gave Julian the third degree. Even though he's not my boyfriend, as I explained repeatedly.

I could tell Julian didn't want to have to explain to the whole world the real reason he was taking up boxing. So he told them that he really wants to get in shape and that they really like boxing at our school. I told them I'm doing it because it was the only extra-curricular left. Parents like words like "extra-curricular."

When they realized there was nothing they could do to stop us from training for our tournament, they backed off a little. A very very very little amount. Which means they're going to keep bugging me throughout the rest of the semester. Fantastic. At least they signed the release form I was supposed to bring back to Ms. Robertson two days ago. I hope I'm not too late for that.

Julian had his form in two days after we got it. When I asked him how his parents felt about it, he just kind of shrugged nonchalantly.

"My dad thinks I'm fat anyway, so he was more than happy to sign," he told me.

For the record, Julian's not fat. Just out of shape. "What about your mom?" There's probably some handbook somewhere that says you shouldn't ask people about their parents, but I'm pretty sure it doesn't apply to friends.

"My stepmom didn't really like the idea," he answered. "She's more into the softer side of protesting things." I must have given him some sort of look because he adds, "I know, it's weird. Sometimes I think I actually take after her much more than my dad."

Okay, I obviously wasn't going to ask him about his real mom, but his stepmom sounds decent.

"Elli!" Dan snaps his fingers in front of my face.

I really need to stop the whole introverted retrospection thing.

"Your turn," Dan says.

Julian gives me an amused smile because he knows how I zone out. I stand in front of them on some seriously old floor mats that Dan has appropriated from who knows where and try to mimic what I saw Julian doing a minute ago. I feel stupid, because all I'm doing is standing there and then throwing a couple of punches. Dan bursts out laughing and I stop to glare at him.

"What's so funny?" I ask him. I can tell Julian is trying hard to cover up his own laughter.

"You look like you're surfing," Dan answers with more mirth in his voice.

I sigh in annoyance and drop my arms. "What do you expect? It's the only sport I've ever done."

"Really?" Julian asks in an awed voice. "That's cool."

I shrug. When you've lived on a beach your whole life, it kind of *becomes* your whole life.

"Well, your whole life is boxing now if you want to be remotely close to good at it," my uncle says, surprising me. Did I speak out loud? And when did he get so bossy?

I frown at him and vow to do better, because I hate when I don't meet expectations. Actually, usually I prefer to exceed them. Yeah, that'll show him.

Uncle Dan stands next to me and attempts to help me adjust my posture. "Just...be normal. No, why are you doing that with your feet? Stand normal."

"I am standing normal!" I snip. "Ugh."

Julian gets up too and I have to consciously keep from rolling my eyes. Now he's on the other side of me in a stance that I swear looks exactly like mine. He puts up his fists and gives me an expectant look and I want to punch him.

"Like this," he says gently.

I suddenly hate how natural he looks, even though I can't help but feel a tiny bit of admiration for him. Still, it annoys me that I feel wrong when he looks so…right.

"I *am* like that," I say to him, my eyes undoubtedly shooting daggers at him. "Exactly like that."

"No, it's—" Jules tries to explain.

I cut him off. "It's not like I have to fight Red, so can't we just focus on you?" Jules and Dan exchange a look. "What am I doing wrong?" I finally ask since neither guy is saying anything.

"Stop standing like you're on a surfboard," Dan says. "Just keep your feet pointed forward and your legs shoulder-width apart."

I look down and realize what it is now. "Oh!" My feet are sideways just like they would be on—you guessed it—a surfboard.

"Much better," Dan and Jules say at the same time. Pride swells inside me but I try not to let it show.

After a while, they give me a little reprieve while Jules works on his punching technique with Dan. Anyway, while they do that I work on my homework, because despite my promise to Jules, I'm not going to let my grades suffer just for boxing.

When I'm not expecting it, they both sit back down and Dan starts speaking. "You guys need to find a way to work on your stamina. I can teach you all the technique in the world, but it won't do any good if you can't last in the ring."

Julian's face, which looked confident a few minutes ago, now looks nervous. I nod noncommittally, because truthfully I'm not that committed. I'm really just here for Julian, but I think it's starting to dawn on him what a huge undertaking he's chosen.

"Like what?" he asks. "You're gonna help us with that too, right?"

Dan puts his palms up. "Hey, you're on your own with that. I can't be with you guys all the time. My recommendation though? Lots of cardiovascular. Anyway guys, I think we're done for today."

Dan's right of course; it is getting late and I'm sure Julian's got some homework he needs to do. And he's right about the fact that we need to take some initiative on our own time. As it is, he's being pretty good about all the free lessons and stuff.

Dan takes off after that, and I sincerely hope he's not going to a bar or something tonight. Just because he told me he would lay off the drinking doesn't mean he actually will, right? Anyway, that leaves Julian and I awkwardly staring at each other in my basement.

In my basement! Alone. I have to get him out. "I'll walk you to the door," I say, which is the politest way of kicking him out.

Julian nods and on the way up, he asks, "What does he mean about cardiovascular?"

I stop dead in my tracks. Julian is probably the smartest kid I know, and I have no doubt that he knows what that specific term means. "You don't know what cardiovascular means?" I ask, dumbfounded.

"I know what it means," he says indignantly, his eyes flashing. Defiance is an increasingly good look for him. "I just don't know what I'm supposed to do about it."

"Oh, sorry," I mumble as I start walking again. "Lots of exercise, I guess. I mean, outside of boxing."

"There's more?" he asks, as if he'd never thought of it.

I give him a sympathetic look. He's not the only one who'll have to work hard. "Sorry," I repeat.

He shakes his head, but the fire is gone from his eyes. "You're becoming more and more Canadian every day," he says to me.

It takes me a while after he's gone to realize that he was referring to me apologizing. But I don't think any amount of apologizing will fix this situation I got us into.

*   *   *

For the last half hour of my shift, Cherry's been hanging out by the sidelines, looking anxious and like she wants to come over to me, but she doesn't. Instead she's ruining her beautiful, sparkly, midnight blue nail polish by chewing on her nails, and darting glances at me then looking away quickly when I meet her eyes. At first I thought she was just being Cherry, but now I'm seriously starting to get worried.

When there's finally a lull in the traffic of people coming to the snack booth, I call her name. She looks at me, startled, and then stalks over. Uh oh. What did I do?

"How are you?" I ask cautiously. I've only spoken to her once since she took me skating, a quick hello between classes. I wonder if she's mad at me because I don't really spend time with her or seek her out.

"Is it true?" she asks, her bright green eyes piercing holes into mine.

"Is *what* true?" I ask back.

"Julian's going to compete against *Red* in the boxing tournament?" she practically squeaks.

Something to know about Cherry is that she's not the squeaky voice kind of girl. She's the husky voice kind, like you'd imagine a jazz singer would sound like talking. My co-worker gives me a look and then suddenly needs to take a smoke break. I'm alone.

"It's true," I finally answer Cherry. I don't see what good it would do to lie about it. She'd find out for sure eventually, just like the entire school probably will.

"Wha—he can't—where were you when this was decided?" She sounds accusatory. I don't like that, especially since it's true.

"Right next to him?" I answer meekly. I never knew Cherry could be so intimidating.

"Why didn't you stop him?" She's verging on hysterical now, so I'm glad there's no one waiting for nachos.

I guess I might as well tell her the truth. "Look, he was standing up for me and for himself. He was about to take hit after hit and so I put a date on their eventual fight, because they both knew it was coming. Now, instead of getting beaten on the spot he has the chance to—"

"Get beaten in front of the whole school?" Cherry fills in for me. Behind her insult, I see a mixture of concern and something unidentifiable. "That guy is huge. Do you have any idea what you've done?"

Okay, to be fair to Cherry, I guess it never occurred to me what would happen if Julian was terrible at fighting and if he lost. I also never really thought about the fact that other people would be watching while he potentially took the beating of his life.

"Cherry," I sigh, "I may have instigated it, but Julian took the challenge. *He's* the one that wanted to do it."

"Then you'll have to get him to back down," she says firmly. But I'm not swayed.

"It's too late to back down," I tell her. "We've already started training. And FYI, he's actually pretty good."

"We?" she asks suspiciously, her eyes narrowing.

"Yes, we. I signed up for the tournament too," I say. Her eyes open and her eyebrows rise to her forehead. A thought occurs to me. "You still like him, don't you?"

"No," she says too quickly. Her expression softens. "But I would care if he got hurt."

It's as much of an admission as I need. I'm about to kill two birds with one stone. "Well, I care about him, too. That's why I'm training with him. Maybe instead of getting mad at me, you should find a way to support him or help him."

"Hmph," she lets out. She turns and is about to walk away when she says quietly over her shoulder, "I'll think about it."

I smile to myself. Step one: make Jules a boxing champion. Step two: make Cherry fall back in love with him.

It's the perfect plan.

*   *   *

After work I check my email—three from friends back home. Still no Kai. Lily's is all about her new boyfriend which is kind of...not as interesting as if we were sitting together giggling about it, if I'm honest with myself. Andrea wants me to know something but doesn't know if she should say it.

Andrea's second email hurts. The thing she wanted to tell me? Lily's boyfriend's name isn't Devin. It's Kai.

I go back up through my emails and delete every single one that Lily has sent me since the move. It's not that I blame her for wanting to be with him, or blame him for moving on. But it feels a little...soon, right? I know he was never technically my boyfriend, but she knew how much I liked him. She could have at least had the decency to just tell me. But she didn't.

CHAPTER TWELVE

I still miss Hawaii, even though I'm annoyed about Lily and Kai. Back home, everything was so much simpler. I didn't have to put on stupid long pants and socks (sometimes two pairs!) every day. I also didn't have to deal with Cherry, who's being completely indifferent to me because she's still hung up over Julian.

I yank a cozy sweater over my head and think about Julian, who it turns out *can* actually box. Much better than I can, too, but I'm trying to not let that bother me. It's important for Julian to learn to box as well as possible in the short time he has. Of course, my uncle has turned into Sifu Bossypants and for some reason, that's highly motivating for Julian.

Me? Not so much. I do not work well under that kind of pressure. The only thing that motivates me is watching Julian get better and better and wanting to have that, too.

It's still cold out, by the way, and I still refuse to wear Adrian's hat. Don't even get me started on him. He used to always be watching me and trying to find dumb excuses to talk to me. Now, nothing. It makes me wonder if it's because I'm an athlete too now. I mean, he must have heard. Practically the whole school knows. Julian and I can tell by the way people whisper when we're around.

It's strange; *that* doesn't bother me, but Cherry and Adrian do. Something strange must have happened on the plane trip over to Canada, because this new Elli is nothing like the old Elli. The old Elli would have felt insecure by all the whispering, but I just brush it off like it's nothing. The old Elli would also ditch people for mistreating her, but this new me? I want to find a way back into their lives, and I don't even know why.

I wince as I push my arms through the sleeves of the sweater. Everything hurts—like literally, my entire body is screaming at me from all the physical activity I've been putting it through. I don't know how Julian's feeling—since he barely shows it, surprisingly—but I can imagine that he's in just as much pain. Of course, that's just speculation. Maybe he's having the time of his life. He and Dan get along pretty well actually.

I'm also tired from going to training, working, and trying to keep up with school. It's not that I want my opponent to win when it comes to the tournament, but at the same time, I'd rather have good grades in school. I'm just saying that being smart lasts a little longer than being an athlete.

I'm glad it's getting a little warmer out, though. It's March now, and I guess the locals think it's "hot" enough outside to wear things like t-shirts? Some of the boys even have shorts on. Most of the girls are prancing around in these light little sweaters that are really cute, but look like they would cause pneumonia or something. A lot of them are even wearing flats and I mean...I'm a forecast kind of girl and I happen to know it's going to snow tomorrow, so that sucks for them I guess.

Today, Mom and Dad are muttering angry things to each other. I have no idea how they got this way. When I was little, they seemed like the perfect couple. They were always holding hands and kissing each other, and showing obvious displays of affection in public and in private. And of course, their love was made complete with their perfect little daughter (other people's words, not mine), and it was all just so...delusional, I guess.

Back then, I always thought I'd want a love like that. You know, to be with that one person that makes you glow, that makes you feel like you're the most special thing on the whole Earth. Now I'm starting to wonder if marriage is such a good idea after all. I mean, look what it turns into over time.

"What is it this time?" I ask as I join them for breakfast before school.

I notice the big fluffy flakes falling outside the window, and I can't wait to sit all smug and cozy in my boots and heavy sweater while the other kids at school suffer.

"What is what?" my mother asks sharply.

"What is it that you're fighting about today?" I clarify. As if that wasn't already obvious to her.

"We're not fighting," she says, with a tone of voice that clearly betrays her. "We just had a disagreement."

Dad gives her a look. "Don't worry about it, Elli."

"I'm not worried," I say defiantly as I pour milk into my cereal bowl. "Why should I be worried about you guys fighting every day? I'm not." And to punctuate my lie, I slam the milk jug back down on the table.

Mom is flustered now, not like when she was arguing with Dad a second ago. It looks like she's trying to come up with something to say, and I'm just glad that for a couple minutes, they've paused their "disagreement."

"This is because of your uncle isn't it?" Mom asks suddenly, just as I take a huge spoonful of my Cheerios.

I try to swallow calmly without sputtering. "What is because of Dan?"

"This attitude you've developed," she says with a frown.

She's *such* a parent.

"What are you talking about?" I ask her. I honestly don't think I have any sort of attitude that I didn't bring with me from Hawaii.

"What *are* you talking about, Shauna?" Dad asks. He sounds a little defensive, and I wonder if it's because he doesn't like what Mom's saying about me or what she's insinuating about his brother.

"You're different, Elli," she says, completely ignoring my dad. "You suddenly want to box, and you're hanging out with boys in the basement, and I—I just don't know about any of this."

I sigh. "Mom, we've been over this. Julian is just a friend and we're training together with Uncle Dan. That's all." I slurp the last of my milk and prepare to leave the table.

"Why are you really doing this?" she says. Her tone of voice stops me cold. There's something she's not saying. But then it comes out. "Did he put you up to this? To…redeem himself or something?"

I open my mouth, but suddenly my dad exclaims, "Shauna!"

"What?" she snaps at him.

"Elli can box if she wants to," dad says. I want to cheer for him, but then he lowers his voice like I still won't be able to hear him and says, "I'm sure it's just a phase. It'll only last as long as this boyfriend does."

Mom makes a strangling sound while I shout, "Dad! This is not a phase and Julian's not my boyfriend. Haven't you been listening to me at all?"

Dad's face reddens as he realizes his mistake. "Elli, I just meant—"

"Whatever, I don't have time for this. I have to go to school."

Both my parents follow me out of the kitchen and into the hallway, watching me as I start to pull my winter clothes on. I'm now fully annoyed with both of them. I thought at least Dad was on my side, but I guess not.

"Don't you want a ride?" Dad asks, having the decency to sound slightly embarrassed.

"No, it's not far." Okay, I've surprised myself by this one, since I would never have said that about walking to school in this weather. But I don't want to be with either of them right now.

"It's cold, Elli," Mom says. "Keep your coat zipped up."

"I will," I say, offering them both a tight smile as I heft up my bag.

The falling snow looked kind of pretty and non-threatening from inside, but as soon as I get outside, I wish I hadn't just declared my independence. It is way too cold for this skinny chick from Hawaii.

As I stamp a trail toward school, I start to reconsider the idea of getting involved in my parents' relationship problems. I mean, I know I'm their kid, but that doesn't mean I have anything to do with what goes on between them, right? On the other hand, I'm kind of glad I told them I'm sick of their yelling. Maybe they'll care *because* I'm their kid.

I'm really glad Julian told me that trick about spraying my boots with that repellent stuff because otherwise they'd be totally soaked right now. You know, Julian's been really nice since he met me, and he hasn't put up much of a fight during our training. I owe him big time. And when I get a chance, I'll repay him. Somehow.

I'm so lost in my thoughts that when a car pulls up to the curb just ahead of me, it startles me and I almost slip on a particularly icy patch of sidewalk. The car looks vaguely familiar but I can't tell why. I'm still trying to figure it out when the front passenger window goes down and Adrian's cute head pops out.

"Elli!" he calls to me. He almost sounds angry and I frown at him. "Do you need a ride? Get in. Seriously, it's way too cold out here for you."

I'm touched by his concern, but considering he hasn't talked to me in a good week or two, I'm not about to just jump at his propositions. Plus, my newfound sense of independence has me hesitating.

When I don't answer quickly enough for his liking, he says, "Come on, it's nice and warm in here."

Funny, how he doesn't even really know me but he knows that one of my most hated things is the stupid cold in Canada. I come up to the car and get in without another word, and I think I actually hear Adrian sigh with relief. He's right about one thing—it's sooo warm in the car.

He turns around and asks, "Why were you walking to school? Do you not watch the forecasts or something?"

I shrug. "I just felt like it."

"And you're not wearing gloves or the hat I gave you because…?" He's peering at me with his warm chocolate eyes and it makes me uncomfortable.

Considering my morning, I'm not exactly inclined to be chewed out by him, so I say, "Is this your mom?"

Of course it must be his mother, but it's fun watching his cheeks go pink when he realizes how rude he's being. The middle-aged woman driving gives me a little appreciative smile in the rear-view mirror.

"Oh yeah, sorry," he mumbles. "Yes, Elli, this is my mom. Mom, this is the girl I told you about—the one from Hawaii."

Whoa, wait. He told his *mom* about me? I'm starting to warm from the inside now.

"Very nice to meet you, Elli," she says. She has the same eyes as Adrian, I realize, but her hair is blond.

"Nice to meet you, too, Mrs. McDuff," I say politely. "Thank you so much for stopping for me. I didn't realize it was quite so cold."

"Now will you tell me where my hat is?" Adrian asks.

I wonder if Mrs. McDuff knows he gave me his hat and how much she knows about me. To tell the truth, the hat is in my backpack, where it always is. I put it in there a couple days after Adrian gave it to me and never took it out. I don't want to admit that though.

"Why, do you want it back?" I ask coyly.

"No," he says, looking at me like I'm crazy. "I told you keep warm.

97

You're supposed to wear it."

"Oh." Welcome back, tongue-tied Elli.

"Do you want this one?" He asks, and points to his head where another plain black hat is sitting.

"It's a nice beanie, but no thanks," I say.

"A...beanie?" he asks, his eyebrows furrowed.

"She means your hat," his mother supplies.

"Of course I mean his hat," I say. "Beanie, hat... What do you guys call it?"

"This is a toque," Adrian says, pointing once again to it so that we're both clear. "Everyone calls them toques. Please don't say beanie around the other kids. They'll think you're nuts."

I laugh as Mrs. McDuff admonishes Adrian for talking to me in such a way. I don't mind. I guess if I have to stay here for the next few years, then I might as well be able to speak like the locals.

"It's all right," I say. "I forgot to bring my American-Canadian dictionary with me today."

Adrian smiles and my heart skips a beat. Literally. I always thought that was a stupid cliché, but it actually just happened and I'm stunned. Mrs. McDuff pulls up to the school and I realize Adrian and I will be walking in together. Like we came together—which we did. But still.

"Thanks again for the ride," I tell Adrian's mom. She smiles sweetly at me and I think that if I were to spend a lot of time with Adrian, I wouldn't mind if some of it were with her too.

"Soo..." Adrian says smoothly.

I throw him a bone. "Thanks for stopping for me, seriously. It was really sweet."

He smiles again, and I realize that if I *were* to spend a lot of time with him, I wouldn't be able to handle seeing his smile more than twice in five minutes.

*　　　*　　　*

Later that day, as I skip rope with Julian (I'll explain that in a bit), I keep thinking about Adrian, and Adrian's smile, and Adrian's mom, and Adrian's hat, and watching Adrian play hockey. After watching hockey practice with Cherry, I had to look up a few games on Youtube to determine whether or not he's a good player, but I've come to the conclusion that he definitely is.

"Elli, is everything alright?" Julian asks me.

"Yeah, why?" I say, all out of breath. At least, I hope he assumes that's why I'm talking like that.

"Because you stopped skipping rope two minutes ago while I was working my butt off," he says with a smirk.

"Sorry," I mumble, picking my rope back up.

"You're just lucky Dan's not here at the moment otherwise you would have gotten yelled at," he says, letting his rope down for a bit.

"He's always yelling at me lately," I say, before I start skipping again.

"He just wants you to do well," Julian says gently.

I huff, because that's pretty much the only response I can make. My uncle managed to convince us that skipping is something every boxer does, but I didn't believe him until I looked it up. Apparently jumping rope helps to build stamina, strengthen leg muscles, trains you to keep light on your feet and have good coordination, and is good cardiovascular. I guess if Muhammad Ali did it, then I should too.

It's not easy though, despite the fact that every little child seems to be able to do it so effortlessly. But to keep up a continuous rhythm takes a surprising amount of work. We're trying to build up to going 20 minutes at a time. Right now I can only manage about four, and Julian, of course, can do a good seven or eight minutes. I just have to keep reminding myself that

I'm doing a good thing by being here for him, regardless of the fact that he's the one who's helping me instead of the other way around.

CHAPTER THIRTEEN

It's busy today at work so there must be some kind of a game on tonight. I wonder if Adrian's playing, but I won't be able to find out until I take a break. In the meantime, I'm serving the masses their masses of junk food.

I actually haven't been doing too badly at saving some money, but here's a shocker: Julian and I have agreed to split the cost of some boxing equipment with Dan. He says he'll pay half if we do, and then maybe after the tournament, we can try to sell them off again if neither of us wants to keep it. I wanted to make enough money to go back to Hawaii for spring break, but with training and working, I know it'll have to wait until school is over. Still, it seemed like a good idea, and I can get some of the money back later. We've decided to start small and just get a punching bag, a dummy, and of course our own helmets and gloves.

There's a girl ordering from me now. She keeps pausing to look straight into my face, like she's trying to figure me out or something.

"Are you all set?" I ask, hoping that that's it.

She nods and then says, "Are you Elika..."

Instead of watching her grapple, I say, "Elikapeka. People just call me Elli."

"So, you're the boxing newbie?" she says, with an unmistakable tinge of admiration in her voice.

I shrug and say uncertainly, "I guess so."

"You should probably come drop by the club at some point, then," she informs me. "We meet every Wednesday and every other Thursday in the weights room."

As soon as she says "weights room," my eyes are immediately drawn to her broad shoulders. She has an athletic build and lean muscles. Her short, brown hair is up in a ponytail, and it occurs to me that I might actually have to fight this girl eventually.

I can feel my forehead creasing as questions form in my mind. "Why would you want to help me?"

She looks surprised at my question. "Because you're new and we're a nice group of a gals... Oh, I know what you're thinking." She probably does, because I probably accidentally thought out loud. "Look, we're not all like Red. Boxing is a fun sport, that can actually be pretty social. But that guy just takes it way too far."

"I see." *What?*

"I do feel sorry for Julian VanderNeen, though," she says, genuinely looking a little sympathetic. Then she giggles. "I'm Emily, by the way. I always forget to introduce myself, always getting to the point too soon. Anyway, I hope you'll drop by, Elli."

She seems so nice that it would be stupid not to take her up on the offer. I nod. "I will. Thanks, Emily."

Later, when I have almost an hour left of my shift, Cherry comes to see me. I dread what she has to say to me, but then I'm surprised when she greets me with a friendly smile. Is this some kind of a trap?

"Ella," she says, leaning against my counter. "Ella, Ella, Ella. Let's go skating when your shift is finished."

It's not exactly an apology so I'm not exactly ready to say yes. "Won't the rink be closed after the game?"

She shrugs and gives me a sly grin. "For the regular people, yeah."

I clear my throat and am saved from having to answer by the person behind Cherry who wants three pretzels, two large cokes, and an order of poutine. Poutine, I've learned, is a heart-attack inducing dish made of fries drowning in gravy and topped with cheese curds. It's disgusting and delicious all at the same time.

When the guy walks away with his order, Cherry turns back to me with an expectant look. Hmm, still not prepared to let her off the hook just yet.

"I guess you don't hate me anymore?" I say to her. My co-worker takes this as her cue to start cleaning the popcorn machine that is the farthest away from us.

Cherry sighs, a guilty expression appearing on her face. "Okay, I'm sorry," she says. "I'm not...a good person, and I overreacted. But then I talked to Julian and he told me about how you stood up for him, then he stood up for you, then suddenly you guys were negotiating a battle and it was like...wow. You know?"

I stopped listening after "I talked to Julian." This is a new development! "You talked to him?" I ask excitedly, forgetting all about being mad at Cherry.

"Yeah," she says, looking a little shy. "But only about that. Don't get any ideas, Ella."

"I have no ideas in my head," I say to her. I hope she doesn't get mad at me again.

"Yeah, sure you don't." She's teasing. That's good. "Anyway, I am sorry. And also, I realized you were right about maybe trying to help instead of stop him. And I want to help you too, which is why you should come skating with me."

I loved and hated skating with her last time, but at the moment, I feel like skating is irrelevant. "How would that help me?" I ask.

"It'll help you build stamina, work on your balance and coordination, plus it's a good workout," she says. Her eyes are shining. She must really, *really* love skating.

"I'm already jumping rope," I huff.

She waves a hand like all the work I've done so far is nothing. "Yeah, but skating is different."

I hesitate, longer than I know Cherry wants me to, and only because it's my own little payback. Then finally, I say, "Alright, I'll come," because obviously I want to go.

As soon as my feet hit the ice, it's like I've completely forgotten everything I did last time. I'm unsteady all over again and I'm starting to wonder why I wasted my time jumping rope at all. But then Cherry takes my hands and starts skating slowly backwards and I feel a little better.

"I'm going to let go now, okay?" she says, when she sees that my feet are where they should be and my legs have stopped wobbling.

"This is kinda fun," I say slowly, because concentrating on words and moving my legs at the same time is hard.

"Yeah it is," she laughs out, as she does some fancy footwork making crisscrossing patterns in the ice.

"You know what else is fun?" I have to move a little quicker now to keep up with her, even though she's still skating backwards.

"What?" she asks. Now she's twirling around and doing sideways moves that probably don't even have names.

"Talking about boys." I'm practically shouting it, since she's gotten quite far away. I'm glad we're alone, because I never would have shouted that to anyone else.

Cherry purses her lips and does some spinning around, as if she's looking through the stands. I try looking too, but I can't quite spin like she can. Besides, there was no one here when we came on the ice. It's fine.

"Okay, which ones?" she asks.

I shrug, and that slight movement almost throws me off balance. "I don't know any boys here but Julian."

"Do you like him or something?" she asks, coming in to skate a little closer to me when she sees me start to flail after shrugging, of all things.

Once I've regained my balance, I tell her honestly, "He's a little geek chic and kind of cute, but no. I don't like him like that. Not like you do."

"Shut up," she mumbles, without the characteristic fire I know she always has. "Are you sure he's the only boy you know?"

I looked down at my skates with the pretense of concentrating on them, but I hesitate a little too long. Suddenly, Cherry's shouting, "McDuff!"

Why is she shouting? What the—?

"Get on the ice!" she calls, and now I see that there is actually someone in the stands. And it's Adrian. Of course.

He looks a little embarrassed to have been caught, and surprised now that Cherry's ordering him around. But then he's sitting down and whipping off his shoes while simultaneously trying to open his gym bag.

"Cherry, what are you doing?" I whisper furiously into her face. "Don't do that. He's just going to bug me about how I'm not wearing gloves." How much of our conversation did he hear? Oh no! He's seen my terrible skating.

"Adrian's a *very* good skater," Cherry says in a loud, over-exaggerated way as we come closer to where he is. She is completely ignoring my protests, as you can see. "But not a very good hockey player."

"That's a lie!" he exclaims, giving Cherry a narrow-eyed, stern look. His fingers, which are expertly tying his skates, never even stop when he looks away. He sees me, smiles, and then finishes tying his skates in record time. At least, I'm sure that's got to be a record.

Suddenly he's skating up to us and Cherry has let go of my hand, and then Adrian's shoving a pair of gloves at me. They each take one of my hands and start moving together as though they had planned on giving me a head rush tonight.

Finally, when I feel as though I'm going to pass out, I yell, "You're going too fast!"

Adrian stops first but doesn't let go of me. Cherry slows down, dragging my hand behind her before finally letting go. She skates backwards toward one of the doors and waves briefly at us. This is payback for nagging her about Julian, I just know it.

"Take care of her!" she calls to Adrian just before shutting the door behind her.

I realize I'm still gripping Adrian's hand tightly so I let go of it. He doesn't complain. We start moving forward again and I try to keep steady so that I don't have to hold on to him.

"So," he says.

"Soo…?" Gah, how long was he watching us? Did I fall? I can't remember if I fell.

"Wanna go, like, really super fast?" he asks me, the enthusiasm in his voice making him sound so young and sweet.

I laugh nervously and answer, "I just tried that, remember? I think I'm good like this, thanks."

"Wanna try going backwards?" he tries again.

He starts taking my hands without really waiting for an answer, and I think, *sure, why not?* "Okay," I say slowly.

He grins as he comes around to face me and then starts pushing me gently backwards. I let out an embarrassing little yelp, which makes him laugh, which makes his dimples magically appear, which makes me almost lose my balance.

"You need to make a little swishing pattern with your feet," he instructs when he sees that I'm not actually moving them at all. "Like, make a V with your heels at the point, and then switch so that your toes are the point. Like this."

He attempts to illustrate this by using his hands, but they just look like fish to me. I stare at him blankly, because what? How am I supposed to get my feet to do that?

"Watch," he says. And then he pushes off backwards, going very slowly so I can watch his heels and toes flip back and forth between each other.

"Oh, I get it," I say.

It doesn't look too hard, so I try it. At first, it's hard to get it coordinated just right, but then when I do, I realize I actually am moving backwards. It's a little bit jerky, but I'm doing it! Adrian gives a delighted little laugh and comes forward to take my hands again. Once he's holding them, my footwork miraculously evens out and we move at a steady pace.

"So, boxing, eh?" He says, after a couple minutes of silent concentration.

He's staring straight at me and doesn't once look down. Oh! It's a question. "Umm, yeah. It sounded like fun."

He inclines his head at my ridiculous explanation. "Right."

"Okay, okay," I say. "I'm doing it for a friend."

"Yeah…so, okay," he says. He drops one of my hands so that he can use his to rub his head, effectively ruffling his dark hair into a sexy mess. "The rumours are that Julian's going to fight Red in the boxing tournament because he's in love with you."

I stop in my tracks and then burst out laughing, because I can't believe that the gossip has actually gone that far. It's also a very incredulous story since that is absolutely the farthest thing from the truth. I realize I've been laughing a little too hard because now Adrian is giving me a frustrated look.

I take a deep breath and then say, "That's ridiculous. Julian fights for himself. I'm just trying to help out."

"So, he's not in love with you?" Adrian asks with a little too much hope in his voice.

I sigh audibly. "I wish people would stop trying to figure out *why* Julian's doing it, and start figuring out *how* to help him do it. I mean, isn't anyone else at school tired of Red picking on other people?"

"Yeah, but have you seen the guy?" he asks. He's still frowning with that little crease between his eyebrows.

"And also," I say, completely ignoring Adrian's dumb question, "Julian's the only person I've ever seen stand up to Red. Other than myself, but they won't let me fight a guy."

Adrian's eyes grow big now. "You can't fight Red. He'll—he'll—"

"Pummel me," I fill in for him. "Yeah, I know. I'm not even that good a boxer. But you know, Julian's actually kind of okay at it."

"Really?" he asks in surprise.

"Yeah, he is," I answer.

"He's not exactly the athletic type," Adrian points out oh-so-helpfully.

"No, he's not," I say. Then I smile at Adrian in what I hope is a very persuasive way. "But he could probably use some help from someone who is the athletic type."

I'm looking all over Adrian's body which, if I haven't mentioned by now, is *very* athletic. He's got broad shoulders, strong hands, muscular legs, and that kind of energy that you only get from working out a lot. He blushes when he notices me noticing him, but recovers quickly.

"I don't know much about boxing," he says. "But...I could try to help him. Maybe do some weight training with him or something."

"Really?" I practically squeal.

He laughs. "Yes, really, if it makes you happy."

"Yes, that would make me really happy," I say. Then I surprise both myself and him by coming forward to give him a little hug. "Thank you so much."

"You're welcome," he says warmly, like he actually means it.

"You know," I say as we start skating forward again, "I don't really know that much about you."

Adrian shrugs with a little frown. "There's not much to tell. I play hockey. It's pretty much the only thing I'm good at." He shrugs again, but I feel like that's just his way of being modest.

"But you're really good at it," I say.

That gets a smile out of him. "Thanks. The truth is that I really love it and even if I were terrible at it, I'd still play. Probably not in my league, but still. What about you? I mean, other than your newfound appreciation for boxing."

"Hockey? No, not me," I joke. He chuckles. I know what he's really asking so I say, "Honestly Adrian? Back home, all I ever did was hang out with my friends and go to beach parties."

Adrian laughs. "What a life."

Either he's being really nice or he didn't read between the lines and figure out that I have zero passions in life. "Really, this is the first time I've taken up a hobby that requires so much…"

"Work?" he fills in with a cheeky grin.

"Yes," I admit with a smile. We've stopped skating or even pretending to skate for the sake of doing something other than just talking.

"Boxing will be good for you, then." He smiles. Then in a very serious voice, he says, "Elli."

"Yes?" I respond, curious at his tone.

"I'm going to kiss you."

Butterflies swarm through my stomach and race up into my heart, clogging my throat until I can barely breathe. I swallow once, and then I say, "If you can catch me."

And then I break apart from him and start skating as hard as I can without thinking too much since I'll trip and fall if I do. And I know he'll catch up to me soon because he can probably skate twice as fast as I can.

A couple of seconds later, he catches me around the waist, spins me around, and starts to lean in. But before his lips reach mine, a loud horn startles us both apart. The Zamboni guy is here, and he's apologetically telling us that we need to clear the ice so he can clean it.

Adrian and I both laugh awkwardly and make our way off the ice. He helps me untie my skates, which is good because my hands are a little cold and shaky now. Neither one of us says anything about our almost-kiss, but instead stick to safer topics. He offers me a ride home, but I decline because Cherry told me she'd take me. I just hope she hasn't forgotten and left already.

Luckily I see her down the hall, hanging out by the vending machines with a book in her hand. Adrian waves to her and she waves back at us.

"I'm going to collect on that kiss," he whispers to me just before he leaves.

Then there are butterflies all over again, and Cherry asks me how it was. I tell her about skating backwards. But not about Adrian and his lips, and how they were so close to mine.

CHAPTER FOURTEEN

Emily has introduced me to the rest of the boxing squad. As soon as they opened their loving arms to me, I wondered why I never tried to find them before now. I mean, they're all so nice. They totally break the athlete girl stereotype.

Emily herself is awesome. While she's the newest member of their group, she seems to be the most friendly and outgoing. All the other girls flock to her, I guess because she's the one that brings them bits and pieces of the outside world. Plus, she brought me along, and they've apparently been dying to meet me.

Now I feel doubly bad for Julian, because it's not like he'll have the chance to hang out with Red like this. I left him with Dan today. My uncle was surprisingly supportive of me doing my own thing with the other female boxers. And then I found out it was because he thought it would be good to check out my competition. I had to remind him that I'm not really in this to win it, at which he scoffed and told me to get back to my rope jumping.

However, I'm happy to say that the wonderful and adorable Adrian has made good on his promise. Yesterday he stopped by our lunch table to tell Julian that he goes running every morning except Thursdays, when he volunteers as a crossing guard for the elementary school down the road. So cute, I know.

Julian, of course, replied, "So?"

For someone who's so articulate and bright, he certainly didn't do himself any justice.

"So," Adrian said, looking at me for the briefest of moments. "Come with me. It's getting nice out now, and it's good for you, and it'll help you with your boxing."

"Oh," Julian said, his eyebrows reaching up to his hairline. "You want me to go with you? Why?"

Now, Adrian could have said any number of things. He could have said he was doing it because I asked him to, or because he wanted to see how dumb Julian would look running. I'm sure Jules was expecting something like that.

But what Adrian actually said was, "Because I want to see you beat Red. And I figure I can help make that happen."

I thought Jules would say no, but he actually agreed. Poor guy. But it really will help him, and I think he knows that. He must. He's a smart guy.

When Adrian went back to his table, Julian said, "That guy's never said more than two words to me. I'm guessing you had something to do with this?" He seemed irritated.

"I asked if he could help," I said with a little shrug, trying not to let my eyes wander to Adrian's retreating backside. "But he wants to help, and he meant what he said."

Jules gave me a sceptical look, but it was obvious he'd already started running with Adrian with this morning. I could tell by the way he carried himself, and how annoyed he was with me. By lunch though, he calmed down enough to tell me about it himself.

112

Oops, there I go zoning out again. One of the girls—Marissa, I think is her name—is trying to ask me something. I have to get more focused before this boxing thing happens.

"I'm sorry," I say, as I wrap tape around my knuckles and wrists. My uncle has been making me do this since the very beginning, describing in vivid detail how badly I could hurt myself if I don't. I'm too afraid to not do it now, and I'm happy to see everyone else around me is also taping their hands.

"I was just wondering how much sparring practice you've had," she says with amused curiosity in her eyes. Most of the other girls are also watching me with that same mixed emotion. They probably all think I'm nuts or something.

"Uh, not much," I answer honestly, keenly aware of how the other girls are starting to tune into our conversation. "Jules and I have been training with my uncle, but he doesn't let us spar together. Something about weight classes?"

There's a round of "Mmhmms" and nodding that makes me feel like I know absolutely nothing about anything. They all seem so informed.

"Yeah, you shouldn't really fight a guy," Marissa says, nodding vigorously. "Even if you were good at it, they would never let you do it in the tournament, and it would throw your whole game off."

"Oh, right, of course," I answer. I want to sound like I know what I'm talking about, and what she said makes sense.

"It's good you came then," Emily says with that ever-present smile of hers. "You can spar with us!"

Agh! I hope I didn't just make that strangled noise out loud. Emily's still smiling at me, so I must not have. Sparring? Sparring with them? With people who know how to spar? I can't.

"Why not?" Emily says, her smile loosening a bit.

Note to self: stop thinking out loud.

"I just—I mean—I don't really know how," I admit. "You know?"

She giggles. "That's why you're here, isn't it? Come on." She slings one arm around my shoulders, her gloved hand resting dangerously close to my face. "We'll warm up a little and then get into sparring. It's a lot of fun, actually!"

Right.

A couple of girls are already skipping. Some of them are punching bags or dummies, or doing weird things with their limbs that I can only assume help them limber up. Marissa has gone to the weight set while another girl—Madison?—follows to spot for her. When Emily notices how my eyes bulge at the amount that Marissa is putting on her barbell, she laughs.

"Normally we don't do lifting and sparring on the same day," Emily explains. "We trade off so that we get equal amounts of training in during the week. And we must always, always have a spotter."

She's very serious about this last point, so I file "always have a spotter" under the very important category of my brain.

"For you, though," she continues, "I would suggest a mixture of weight lifting, technique exercises, and sparring *every* time you come in. Only because, well...you know."

She glances at me, like my whole body, and I get it. She wants me to be in proper shape for the tournament and it's clear to her that I'm not.

"I'm not going to do very well with this, am I?" I say.

She flicks a hand at me and then reaches down to grab a stray jumping rope off the ground. "You'll be fine," she says as she hands me the rope. Even here I can't escape the endless skipping. "As long as you work hard."

Ah, and there it is. This is only going to work if I work hard. Darn. I guess there's no escaping it. If I truly want to be supportive to Julian, I have to want to win as badly I want him to win. Alright then. I guess it's time to get down to business.

The girls are showing me some warm ups that are supposed to be specific to female boxers, but I feel like that's their way of making me feel included. It's actually kind of nice to be treated that way. Although at the same time, I feel like they're all so much more hardcore than me.

Finally, when I'm all loose and comfortable, Marissa asks me, "How would you like to spar?"

"Oh, I, uh—" As I struggle for words, I notice I'm catching the attention of the others again. Will it always be like this?

"That's just a nice way of saying get your butt up here," Denise says. She's this really tough-looking chick with cornrows in her black hair. She already has a helmet on. I'm scared for my life.

Marissa sees the look I must have on my face and laughs. "Don't worry, Denny's really easy on the noobs."

"If you say so," I say, trying not to visibly tremble.

Denny hands me a helmet and then grins. After I take the helmet, she knocks her gloved hands together in a typical "I'm ready, are you ready?" gesture that feels familiar even though I haven't been boxing all that long. Must be from the movies or something.

Someone helps me put my gloves on, and then I get shoved into the small-scale ring that's been set up for the boxing season. Denny starts dancing on her feet and I start doing the same. This I know for sure: always keep moving. As my uncle told me, it keeps your opponents from being able to hit you.

Denny throws a punch and I'm proud of myself for dodging it. Until I realize that it was a fake and she's now hitting me from the other side. Ugh. Get it together, Elli. I throw an admittedly weak left cross when I see an open spot, and it lands! Not hard, but still.

Suddenly the other girls are cheering from me, which provokes some taunts from Denny. The girls are all trying to lead me into different moves, but it's hard to concentrate on their voices and what I'm doing at the same time. I miss a block and my head snaps to the side. I know Denny's taking it easy on me, and it's not a hard hit, but it's still a hit. I'm glad I have the helmet now.

"You really gonna let me take you down, Hawaii?" Denny asks, her cocky little grin still in place.

That is it. I'm throwing my gloves down!

Not literally though, because I still need them.

Suddenly, with a strength I didn't know I had, I rush at Denny. I noticed she keeps her gloves very close to her face, but it leaves her elbows too far apart. So I fake to the open spot between them and then when she reaches down to block—I knew she'd do that, too—I move quickly enough to land a hit on the right side of her head.

She looks surprised at first, and then her eyebrows lower. Now she knows she can pump it up, which means I better be able to, as well. She hits me, harder this time, on my left side.

"Keep your elbows in!" Someone yells to me.

Right, elbows in. Fists by my cheeks. Dodge that punch! Phew, I did it.

After a good combination of dodging and blocking, I can tell Denny is starting to get bored. She knocks her knuckles against mine a couple times, a taunting move that means I'm supposed to do something.

"Come on, hit me, Elli," she says.

She almost sounds kind when she says it. So I feel a little bad when I take this opportunity to get in a swift uppercut to her chin. Her head tilts back, but she recovers quickly and then laughs deeply, because she's excited to get me moving again.

We spar like this, back and forth for a few more minutes. I do a lot of blocking, because I'm not very confident with my punching, and also because I'm afraid of being hurt. But I land a few good ones, which throws the other girls into fits of cheering. By the end, I know I've definitely lost, but they're all still shouting my name.

"Okay, okay," I finally say, when I'm drenched in sweat, my muscles are screaming, and I can barely move. "I think I'm done."

I'm already standing hunched over with my hands resting on my thighs. Denny drops her stance and stops bouncing. With another cheery grin, she comes over to me and helps me out of the ring. Who knew boxers could be so nice?

"You did good," she says, as Emily starts taking off my gloves.

"Yeah, that was amazing, Elli," Emily says, excitement running rampant through her voice.

I'm breathing heavy and I feel disgusting, but I have to admit: it feels kind of...good. And addictive. Even without being the winner, the rush of boxing is totally worth the effort it takes to get here.

"That was a lot of fun!" I say suddenly. The other girls laugh and nod, like they knew all along that this is what would happen.

They break apart again to do their own things and I decide that maybe I should check the time. I have to work later tonight, and I need a shower first. When I get my cell phone out of my backpack, I see that I've missed four calls from Julian, which is concerning to say the least, since he never calls me.

I call him back and he answers on the first ring. "What's wrong?" I ask, because I'm sure something's wrong.

"I don't know where Dan is," he says. He sounds a little out of breath. "I went to your house and your parents were gone, and I guess Dan was, too."

"Are you sure?" I ask, my mind spinning with possibilities. "Did you try the back door?"

"Of course," he huffs. "I waited for like twenty minutes. That's why I called you. To see if you knew if he needed to cancel or something."

"Not that I know of," I answer. Where could he be? I hear someone yell something in the background on Jules' end. "Where are you?"

"Well, since I figured training wasn't happening today, I decided to go for a run instead. I'm with Adrian."

"Oh," I say, and I know my voice holds much more warmth in it than it should.

"Yeah, yeah," he says dryly. "Your boy's being all nice to me. Look, I'll catch you later, okay? Adrian's yelling at me to pick it up."

"Okay," I say. Then, because I feel like I should, I add, "I'm sorry. I'll try to find Uncle Dan. Tell Adrian I said hi."

"Hah."

Now I'm not sure whether to stick around here with the girls or try to find Dan. I guess I should see where he is. I mean, I know he's been training us for free, and maybe he just wanted a day off. But really, I'm worried that he's somewhere seedy, drinking his weight in alcohol like he promised he wouldn't do. I don't like the idea.

I reluctantly tell the girls I have to go, which is the truth anyway. I'm very grateful that they've taken me in and I hope they know that. Maybe they'll be just as nice to me when the actual tournament comes around. But I gather it's not likely, based on how the other girls are currently sparring together.

Now to find Dan.

CHAPTER FIFTEEN

I call my uncle three times, but every time it goes straight to voicemail. I'm beyond mad now, but I'm also a little concerned. That's when I remember that maybe, if I'm lucky, Dan might have left his phone's GPS running, and I could track him down that way.

Opening up the map on my phone, I hope for the best. I wait for a really long time while it finds me and then... Bingo! Dan's signal shows up somewhere close to the mall, which means he's not too far from the school. I think about calling him one more time, but opt for just surprising him instead. My only hope is that he isn't at some bar or something.

I follow my map diligently until it stops in front of a cozy-looking restaurant. When I go inside, the seating hostess offers to seat me, but I wave her off, telling her I'm looking for a friend. She gives me a slightly disgruntled look behind her smile and I walk past her, scanning the half-full dining room.

I see my uncle sitting at a corner table with a woman and start walking toward him without thinking. When I'm halfway there, it hits me: he's with a woman. Crap. He's on a date. I know I can't interrupt that, but before I get a chance to turn and run, Dan looks up and makes eye contact. He gives me a little frown but then half stands and calls my name.

I walk over, surreptitiously eyeing the woman sitting across from him. At least, I hope I'm being surreptitious. She looks young, maybe younger than him. Ridiculously long chestnut hair that's got a perfect curl to it, big blue eyes, and a mouth that's twisted into a little amused smile as she eyes me right back.

"Elli, what are you doing here?" Dan asks, trying hard not to sound annoyed.

My face is flushed and I hope they assume it's from walking out in the cold. "I didn't mean to interrupt you," I say, casting the woman an apologetic look. "But I was worried when you didn't show up for training with Julian."

"Training?" Dan sounds confused. "I'm out for lunch right now…"

There's a clock on the far wall and I look at it pointedly. "It's 4:30," I say.

"Crap," Dan says, sounding genuinely remorseful. "Well, what is he doing now?"

I shake my head. "He's out running with friends. Working on his cardio and stuff."

"He has running friends?" Dan can't resist the barb.

I roll my eyes. "*I* have running friends." I glance again at the woman he's with, who smiles at me like she's trying to figure out who I am and what we're talking about.

Dan notices and says, "Sorry I'm being rude. Liz, this is my niece, Elli. Elli, this is Liz. She's my," there's a slight hesitation before he finishes with, "Get Dry sponsor."

"Oh!" I say surprised. So, was it a date or not? Adults are weird. I stick my hand out. "Very nice to meet you. Sorry again for barging in."

"It's no problem," Liz says in one of those soft voices that you can only expect from someone with such large doe eyes. "You're the future boxer I've heard so much about."

My face flushes all over again. "Well, I'm not that great at it," I tell her shyly. "I'm really just doing it for my friend."

"I think that's really sweet," she says, and I get the feeling she knows more about it than I thought.

"Yeah," I say slowly. "Anyway, I'm gonna get out of your hair now. Go find some…training to do or something."

Dan winks appreciatively. "I'll see you later, kid."

I leave the restaurant feeling awkwarder than life, but glad that Dan was so good about the fact that I just dropped in on his date. To try to put it out of my mind, I call Julian to see if he still wants to come over and do some training with me.

Unfortunately, he says, "Nah, sorry. My grandparents are coming over for dinner soon and then I have homework to do."

"That's okay," I say, and I'm sure he can hear the disappointment in my voice.

"Hey, you can always ask your boyfriend," Julian teases. "I don't think he actually does homework."

"He's not my boyfriend," I mutter, even though I know Julian won't let up anyway.

"Look, Elli, I gotta go," Julian says, totally ignoring my protest like I knew he would. "But I'll see you tomorrow, okay?"

"Alright," I sigh before ending the call.

It occurs to me that I still have to get home somehow before I go to work. But surprisingly, it doesn't feel too cold out so I decide to walk. Of course, then I realize that "not too cold out" only applies for the first two minutes, then it goes back to freezing. Oh well, I've made my choice and I'll stick with it.

*　　　*　　　*

Things are different at school. I've been trying to put my finger on what exactly has changed and I think I've got it. It's definitely the way people are interacting with Julian. I mean, it's perfectly normal for kids to say hi in the hallways between classes, do a little catching up, or at least offer some form of acknowledgment. But not for Julian. No one ever pays attention to him.

Until recently, that is. First it was little head nods from some of the jocks, of all people. Then some of the girls who aren't the populars but aren't unpopular started whispering in the hallways when he was near, giggling and even saying hi to him. Now I'm watching a group of cheerleaders eyeing him while we eat lunch.

"Hey Jules, have you noticed a slight shift in your popularity recently?" I ask him, as one of the cheerleaders gets out of her seat, her eyes on the back of Julian's head. I think her name is Lindsay.

He looks up from his textbook—yeah, he's getting started on homework at lunch again—briefly and says, "No, why?"

I just smile my amusement as Lindsay finishes her trek across the cafeteria and plops down next to Julian. "Hey," she says.

"Hi," Julian greets back, staring at Lindsay like she has two heads.

Lindsay smiles and it almost looks genuine, too. Putting her hand out, she says, "Give me your phone."

Julian's eyebrows draw inwards, probably as much as mine, and says in a shocked voice, "What?"

Lindsay giggles and touches his shoulder. "Trust me."

For some reason that is beyond me—okay, let's be honest, it's totally about her beautiful red hair and that cute laugh—Julian actually gives Lindsay his cell phone. Once she has it, she takes out her own phone that was hiding somewhere in the recesses of her cleavage, which draws Julian's eyes downwards for a brief moment before he realizes what he's doing. He glances at me with a slight blush and confused expression and I just shrug.

"What are you doing?" he asks as Lindsay puts their phones back-to-back.

"You'll see," she answers mysteriously, her gaze glued to her phone. "In just…10 seconds…and 5…and here you go," she says brightly, handing Jules his phone back.

"What'd you do to it?" he asks sceptically.

Lindsay laughs again. "Nothing. The girls and I made a playlist for you," she tells him, gesturing to the table where most of the cheerleaders eat together. "For your workouts," she clarifies. Then she does that shoulder-touching thing one more time before she gets up and leaves.

Julian's eyes follow her sashaying butt all the way back to her table where the cheerleaders smile and wave at him. His eyebrows draw inwards again, like he doesn't trust them.

"Let me see that," I say to him. He's still looking at the table full of girls, so I take his phone to look at it.

The playlist is entitled Roar and features, unsurprisingly, Katy Perry's "Roar" as the first song. I scan the rest of it. "Eye of the Tiger," "Titanium," "Harder, Better, Faster, Stronger," "The Rocky Theme Song." These are some good songs, I have to admit. I thought they'd all be girly, but they're not.

"Cute," I say, as I pass the phone back to Julian.

"Is this your doing?" Julian asks pointedly as he peruses the playlist.

"Me? No," I say. Has he not noticed how differently people are acting towards him? I couldn't have gotten a whole school to just spontaneously do that. "I had nothing to do with that. Or with the way those girls over there are eyeing your biceps."

Julian looks in the direction I'm pointing, and the group of girls I mentioned quickly looks away from him. He snorts. "What girls? I mean…what biceps?"

"These ones, sillyhead." I reach across the table and grab hold of his upper left arm encased in what used to be a fairly loose t-shirt.

My first thought: *whoa.*

Second thought: *are my biceps getting bigger too?* I immediately let go of his arm to feel my own. Nope, still pretty skinny.

"Ella."

"Yeah?" I'm still trying to find my muscles.

"What are you doing?"

I look up at Julian and he's smirking at me. I smirk back. "I wanted to know if my muscles have grown as much as yours."

"They do seem to be bigger than when I first met you," he says like he really means it.

"Aww, thanks," I say.

Julian smiles. "Is it time for math yet?"

I frown at him. "There's no taking the geek out of you, is there?"

He just laughs and shakes his head.

When he gets up and slings his backpack on, I can't help looking at his arms one more time because seriously, *whoa.*

*   *   *

Mom and Dad had another fight. When I get home from work, they're both in the living room, Mom reading a book and Dad perusing a newspaper. They aren't even talking to each other, but I can tell by the tension in the air that something's up. I don't know whether to ignore it or ask about it. I opt for ignoring it because asking is just awkward.

"Hey, Kiddo," Dad greets me.

I give him a look. "Dad, I'm not a kid anymore. I mean, come on. I'm a boxer now!"

I get into a half-decent stance and throw a couple of fake punches in his direction. Dad laughs and pretends to cower in fear of my might. It makes me smile.

"You're looking pretty good, Elli," he says. "And what about that boyfriend of yours?"

My heart skips a beat as my thoughts immediately jump to Adrian, who isn't at all my boyfriend. But Dad hasn't even met Adrian so how would he know that Adrian could almost possibly be boyfriend material? And then it dawns on me. He's asking about Julian.

"Daaaad," I drawl with an eye-roll as I sit down next to him on the couch. "Julian is most definitely not my boyfriend. But since you asked, he's actually doing very well. He might just have a shot at the tournament."

My mom scoffs. It's her way of joining the conversation.

"Hmm," Dad says. "I wonder what Dan's putting him through to get him ready on time. Not that my brother's exactly in shape either."

I perk up a little. "You could watch us train sometime. I'm sure Jules wouldn't mind. You should see, too, Mom." I give her my most fetching smile in hopes that maybe she'll pretend that she likes me at least a little.

Mom opens her mouth and I know she's about to decline my offer when Dad says, "Come on, Shauna. This is something Elli wants to do. We should support her."

Mom glares at Dad for a very tiny second before saying in a bright tone, "I was about to say that I would *love* to watch you train, Elli."

"*Really?*" I squeak out.

"Sure, why not?" Mom answers airily likes it's no big deal. But I know it is to her, because she doesn't really want me to box.

"Oh, Mom, I'm getting so good at it," I tell her. And I really mean it. I want her to know that I like it and that's why I'm sticking with it.

Mom just smiles.

"So," I say lightly. "What were you fighting about this time?"

"Nothing," they both say at the same time.

I decide not to push it. It's not my place anyway. "Okay, well, I'm tired. I'm just going to go do my homework and then go to bed."

I kiss them both goodnight and they look at me strangely. Now that I think about it, I guess I haven't actually kissed them goodnight in a long time.

I take my backpack upstairs, close my bedroom door, and then pull Adrian's hat onto my head. Like I do pretty much every night. I know, it's a little creepy. And totally unnecessary now that the snow has stopped falling. But at the same time…I can't help it. I like the way it feels.

And I like the way it feels to know someone who is totally cute and awesome likes me enough to give me his hat and not ask for it back. And I like the way it doesn't make me think of Kai.

CHAPTER SIXTEEN

Dan has been pushing us hard lately, which hasn't left me much time to work on getting Jules and Cherry together. I know, I know—priorities. I realize the tourney is in a month, but it's not like I'm the one who has to fight Red. Really, my time could be better spent doing something else. Instead I'm here—

"Pick up your feet, Elli!" Dan barks at me.

I sigh and jump higher over my jump rope. Julian gives me a sympathetic look, presumably because he knows Dan is much harder on me than on him. Or at least it feels like that.

"Pick up that attitude, too, Elli," Dan adds in a *slightly* softer voice.

I give him the cheesiest smile I can muster and skip lightly, adding a little flare in my shoulders for good measure. Dan laughs, which makes me smile for real.

After we've sufficiently warmed up, I get a little break while Dan works with Julian. Dan's trying to teach him as many moves as he can in such a short time; we've moved beyond jabs, crosses, and uppercuts. Lately we've been working on more complicated things like lay backs, parries, and the bob and weave.

My favourite technique is called "the slip" and surprisingly, I seem to have gotten a better hang of it than Julian. The slip involves getting to know your opponent so that you can predict where and when their next punch will be. Then you can dodge it by the slightest bit before striking hard. Like I said, I've gotten pretty good at it. Julian on the other hand...

"You're dodging too late," I tell him gently, trying to be helpful. He gives me a wary look.

"It's hot in here," he mutters in annoyance, like that's his problem right now. He slips his shirt off which is very uncharacteristic of him since he's more modest than an Amish school girl.

Then my jaw drops. Because where I expected to find flab and rolls there are now pecs and a six pack. His abs aren't exactly washboard material, but they are pretty tight. I'm impressed and a little jealous and also a little embarrassed when Julian realizes I'm staring.

"What?" he snaps, still annoyed.

"Nothing," I respond, immediately dropping my eyes to my history textbook which I'm only pretending to read.

There's a knock on the door to the basement and I look up. My dad walks in and his eyes narrow in on Julian. My mom follows him in and gives Dan a scowl in greeting, then glares at Julian's bare chest.

"What's this?" Dan asks with a disapproving frown.

"Elli invited us," Mom says smugly, taking a seat on the one old couch we have down here.

Dan looks at me sharply, to which I reply, "I thought they'd like to see me in action, you know?"

"To watch you jump rope and throw punches at a dummy," Dan says with one eyebrow raised.

"No," I half-mumble. I look up at Julian. "Come on, Jules, let's spar. Just a little."

His eyebrows draw in the slightest bit and he looks at Dan for confirmation, which kind of annoys me, to be honest. I mean, Jules is *my* friend after all. Dan sighs and shakes his head disapprovingly. But then he helps me into my gloves before taking a seat on the arm of the couch next to my dad.

"Just take it easy on her," Dan warns Julian as we take our stances across from each other.

"You don't have to do that," I mutter under my breath, giving my friend a cocky smirk. I knock his gloved hands—a gesture I learned from the girls a while ago. It's some sort of a greeting, I guess.

Julian smiles back at me and we begin. It's kind of weird that we've never actually sparred together no matter how much we've trained together. And no matter how much time I've spent with him at school, no matter how well I think I know him, I'm about to discover another side of Julian.

A very different side. This side is all skilled determination. If I didn't know better, I would never have guessed that Julian is a soft-spoken bookworm. He moves quickly, his jabs are light and effective and his footwork is almost perfect. Again, I'm struck with mixed feelings of admiration and jealousy. I'm also a little annoyed because I know he's not giving me all he's got.

But it's okay, because I know his weakness. The slip. I let him keep throwing a few weak punches at me, blocking them as best I can. And then I see my opportunity—he's getting bored, so I goad him a little until he charges up for what I know is his best move.

I dodge it easily and now that I'm out of his way, he's in mine and I take a swing right at his head. Julian is so surprised by the force of my hit that he drops his arms and stares at me. He realizes his mistake a second too late because I'm not finished fighting yet, and so I give him a swift uppercut that nearly knocks him off balance.

I probably should have warned him first, but Julian should have known better. Plus it feels kind of good to hear my parents cheering for me, Dan praising me and scolding Julian, and Julian staring at me with a look of annoyed wonderment.

"Alright, you got me fair and square, Ella," Jules says with laughter in his voice. "But don't expect it to happen again."

"Then don't drop your arms again," I tell him, keeping my hands next to my face.

So Julian puts his fists back up and we start again. He's better than me by far, and he's definitely holding back still, but I'm not too bad. I'm just glad for him. I really am. Because if he'd been terrible at boxing then I would have felt even worse about the mess I got him into. But now—now I think he might be able to beat Red.

We didn't really call a winner (although it's totally him) before Julian stops and says he really should get home to do some homework. I should feel bad about his grades because I know he hasn't had as much time to devote to school and he's probably never gotten less than an A+ or something. But really, all I feel is pride. I'm proud that the same focus and determination he has for academics can be applied to athletics too.

After Julian leaves and Dan skitters off to wherever he goes in the evenings, I sit with Mom and Dad in the living room. We are, of course, doing our own things—Dad's reading the newspaper, Mom's working on some take-home stuff, and I'm doing homework. But for the first time in a long time, there is a little peace that settles in. It's nice.

"Your form is good, Elli," Dad says without taking his eyes off his newspaper.

I glance up at him. I know he's trying to compliment me without embarrassing me so I say, "Thanks," and really mean it.

"I'm surprised Dan even remembers boxing," Mom comments, all the while filling in little notes on her pages with red pencil. "Did he ever box after…?"

Dad shakes his head and answers, "Nope," before Mom finishes her question, leaving me to wonder what happened before *after*.

They both fall silent, so after a moment, I ask, "Wait, what happened? Did he get hurt or something?"

Dad hesitates before saying, "I shouldn't say…"

But Mom obviously doesn't care because she blurts out, "Your uncle choked up during a huge tournament and lost to a really lousy competitor."

Whoa.

"Shauna," Dad says wearily.

"What?" she retorts. "Don't you think Elli deserves to know why her coach hasn't boxed in over fifteen years? Even I knew that Dan was an amazing boxer. He should have been able to beat all the competition and he didn't."

"Why not?" I ask. "Was it nerves or something? He doesn't strike me as the nervous type."

Mom shakes her head. "He's not. His girlfriend broke up with him the day before and he came to the tournament drunk. He never boxed after that, but he did keep drinking."

Dad sighs and puts his newspaper down. "That's not exactly how it went. For one thing, Chantal didn't break up with him—she cheated on him. And for another, the day of the tournament was the anniversary—" he cuts himself off just before his voice rises to the level of yelling and takes a deep breath. "The anniversary of Tim's death. That was his best friend growing up," he adds for my sake.

Double whoa.

"That's so sad!" I say, and I really mean it.

"Don't say anything to him about it, though," Dad says.

"And especially don't mention Chantal," Mom adds. "He can do so much better."

Mom's defending him now? Weird. "No, of course not. Out of curiosity though, what day was that?"

"May…" Dad looks at Mom, who rolls her eyes.

"Twenty-first," she finishes for him.

"May twenty-first?" I ask queasily. *No, no, no.* "You don't think he still has any hang-ups about that date, do you?"

I hear "No," and "Probably," at the same time.

"Why do you ask?" Mom asks.

"Oh, it's just…that's the day of our tournament." I don't mean for it to come out sounding selfish. I just don't want it to be another bad experience for Uncle Dan.

"I'm sure it's fine, Elli," Dad says with a small smile. "Don't think about it. Just do your best and you'll do him proud."

"Thanks, Dad."

*   *   *

The next night I find myself ice skating with Adrian again after hockey practice is over. I didn't even see Cherry, but I know she had something to do with our private ice time. It's kind of nice of her actually. I'm sure Adrian appreciates the extra practice time, too.

Adrian's being super nice again. When I fall flat on my butt, he doesn't even laugh. He just helps me up and gives me one of his ridiculously dimply grins which almost makes me fall over again. It makes me wonder why he hasn't asked me out since our almost-kiss. I mean, don't almost-kisses mean anything these days?

"I heard some rumours about Neener," Adrian says after we've been skating silently for a few minutes.

I discovered that "Neener" is a name a lot of kids at school call Julian, and is usually paired with "Keener." I think some of them even mean it endearingly now, but I don't think it's a nice name and I don't like that Adrian's using it.

"What kind of rumours?" I ask. "And don't call him that."

Adrian lifts an eyebrow at me and frowns a little and I swear his frown is almost as beautiful as his smile. "Just, you know, you guys..."

"Us guys...?"

"Training together and stuff..."

"Training together," I say flatly. "That's not a rumour, that's a fact."

"Yeah, but like..." he hesitates and I already know I don't like what's coming. "There's nothing more going on?"

I stop skating just to sigh because I cannot even comprehend that he's asking me that after everything. After our private little skate sessions, after he gave me his hat that I haven't given back, after our almost-kiss. Why is he asking me that?

"How many times are you going to ask me that question before you believe my answer?" I ask him, trying not to sound as hurt as I feel. I mean, it's not like we're a couple or anything, but I know he likes me and he should know I like him by now, right?

"I know. I'm sorry," he says hastily. "It's just—you spend so much time with him."

"I spend a lot of time reading textbooks too, but you're not suspicious of them," I tell him, trying for levity.

"You don't eat lunch with your textbooks," he says. Is he actually sulking? "Your textbooks don't make you laugh."

"He's not allowed to make me laugh?" I ask incredulously. "For a guy who's not even my boyfriend, you're being oddly possessive."

"I'm not—" Adrian cuts himself off and exhales loudly. "I just think you should tell me right now if I should even bother asking to be your boyfriend or not."

"*That's* what you were leading up to?" I practically shout into the empty rink.

"Couldn't you tell?" he asks, giving me that adorable frown again that I want to smack right off his face.

I shake my head. "You want to know why I spend so much time with Julian, why I always eat lunch with him? Because when I first started going to your school, he was the one that made friends with me. He made me laugh when I hated my life. And he stood up to Red *with* me and *for* me. If you can't accept that…then no, I don't think you should ask. I'm sorry."

I'm not even sure I mean the apology, but it seems like the Canadian thing to do before I clumsily skate away from Adrian and his messy hair and cute dimples and silly little accent.

CHAPTER SEVENTEEN

Walking into the cafeteria today is like walking into a parallel universe. Julian is surrounded by people. I was only like a minute late leaving my last class and this is what happens. Kids from all different cliques are sitting around his table, talking amongst themselves but also including him in their various conversations. I catch Adrian pointedly ignoring Julian and his new posse.

For the first time since my first day here, I don't know what to do with myself. I mean, it's cool that so many people want to hang out with Julian, but I don't see an empty chair anywhere near him. And to be perfectly honest, he doesn't even seem to miss me.

I stare for a minute longer until I hear a voice beside me say, "Sickening, isn't it?"

It's Cherry. "What is?" I ask, feigning ignorance. I turn towards her and see that her hair is now electric blue which goes great with the black studs in her ears and eyebrow.

She points with her chin in Julian's direction. "The clinging pop culture masses. They always find the next best thing."

"What's wrong with them wanting to hang out with Julian?" I ask, as I head toward the nearest empty table.

"What's wrong with it?" she repeats, flopping down into one of the chairs. "Tell me, why do you like Julian?"

I wonder if she's trying to trap me, trick me into admitting something that's not true. But that's not like Cherry and I don't think she meant it that way. So I answer, "He's nice, smart, determined. Makes a great punching bag."

Cherry doesn't laugh. "He's hilarious, he always knows the right thing to say, he has almost every single issue of *Captain Canuck*, he's brilliant, and he's so genuine it hurts."

"What's your point?" I ask, though I'm dying to know what *Captain Canuck* is.

"My point is that those people over there don't know Julian," she says. "Not like you do and not like I do. They're all into him now because he's got muscles and an interesting story. But as soon as that fight is over, no matter the outcome, they'll slowly start to forget about him until he fades into the walls all over again. He deserves better than that."

Well, this is almost heading in the right direction. But I feel like there's more that she's not saying. "Can you blame them?" I ask. "He *does* have an interesting story and he *has* changed dramatically. Why not let him enjoy it while it lasts?"

Cherry gives me a look that lets me know that what I said was completely off the mark. And then it hits me. It's not them she's mad at; it's him. But why?

I must have asked out loud because the next thing I know, Cherry is bursting out, "Because I liked him when he was just him. Before the working out, when he was cool in his own way. And he stood me up! But for these punks—I just don't get it."

She's trying to hide it, but I can see tears lurking beneath that heavy eye makeup. She's hurt and I'm not sure how to fix it. I'm not even sure if it can be fixed.

"Oh, Cherry," I say kindly. "I'm so so—"

"Do you see what you've turned him into?" she asks me, her eyes narrowing to a glare. "All for some stupid boxing tournament? All to prove some stupid point?"

Wait, I thought she was mad at Julian. But now she's mad at me?

"Look, I didn't turn him into anything." I try not to sound defensive, but I don't like her tone of voice or the things she's saying. "He did this all on his own. He chose to take up boxing, he chose to make a point. He's worked really hard for this and if you were really that into him, you'd be proud of how far he's come in such a short time."

"Proud?" Cherry says, the hurt still evident on her face. "How can I be proud of something so shallow, and stupid, and fake? How can I be proud when I know he's just going to get hurt—by Red and by all those people who suddenly want to be friends with him?"

"You still don't believe in him, do you?" I ask. I honestly can't figure out where Cherry's feelings for Julian stand.

"Believing in him isn't going to make him win," Cherry answers hotly.

I give her a hard stare and I know the instant it works. She shrinks back a little. "Look around you, Cherry," I say in my strongest voice. "Those aren't just jocks over there with Julian. There are all kinds of kids— nerds, art kids, band geeks, jocks, popular and unpopular kids. And if I do recognize them correctly, there are some who have and others who have not been bullied by Red. They all want to be with the one person in this school who will actually stand up to Red. Can't you see? Julian already has won."

Cherry's mouth drops open, but I don't stick around to see what she has to say. I stalk off and head towards my locker because I really have nowhere else to go since lunch is only halfway through.

Julian finds me a few minutes later and I'm surprised that he's broken away from the crowds. He smiles at me and I can't help smiling back.

"Hey, Ella," he says gently, dropping down onto the floor next to me. "Are you okay? I hope your parents weren't all weird about us sparring yesterday."

"Oh, no," I said. "I wasn't even thinking about that and actually my parents were pretty cool about it."

"That's cool." He can tell something's up, I know it. "So…I saw you talking to Cherry just now. I hope you maybe put in a good word for me?"

I shake my head. Well, technically I put in a lot of good words for him, but it wasn't like that. "Sorry, but we were actually kind of arguing."

"Oh," he says disappointedly.

"But it was about you, if that helps."

He lifts an eyebrow. "How is that supposed to help?"

"I don't know."

He's silent for a moment, then he asks timidly, "Soo…what did she say about me?"

"Oh, Jules." I sigh and look him straight in the eye. "She likes you a lot but she doesn't know what went wrong between you two and now she feels out of place because you prefer to spend your time with other people instead of her." Julian's eyes drop to his lap and I add, "I don't really get what happened either."

Julian takes in a deep breath and out rushes, "I just panicked, okay? First, I couldn't believe she would ever want to go out with someone like me. Then when I finally convinced myself that yes, the coolest girl in school could maybe possibly be attracted to *me*, of all people, I psyched myself out. I got all obsessed over the potential for our new relationship, but then it occurred to me that I am just not good enough to be Cherry's boyfriend, and that when it ended, it would be really messy because I would probably cry more than she would and beg to have her back and she would maybe stomp all over my heart when she realized what a total dork I really am and that she could do so much better. So in the end, I did us both a favour and made sure that first date never happened."

My eyes are probably huge. I can't believe all of that was going through his head. "Are you kidding me?" Of course he wasn't, not by the look on his face. "Okay, look, this is fixable. But you're going to have to be brutally honest with her and hope that she doesn't think that's the dumbest thing she's ever heard."

"Is it really that dumb?" he has the nerve to ask.

"For you, yes," I answer. "For a 12-year-old girl, no."

He gives me a withering look and I laugh.

"I promise we can fix it," I repeat.

"Don't make promises you can't keep, Ella," he says in that timid voice again.

"I *promise*."

*   *   *

I see Adrian coming towards me at the end of the day, but I ignore him and skitter away. I'm not ready to talk to him yet—I'm not even sure what I would say. Besides, I'm already late to practice with the girls. They promised to help me with more weight training today, even though I kind of like sparring more than anything else.

Denny, Marissa, Madison, and Emily are already there. Denny and Maddy are already warming up in their makeshift ring while Marissa and Emily are spotting each other while lifting weights. Denny grins at me and I know she's dying for a chance to spar with me to see how far I've gotten in my training. With the tourney coming up soon, the girls have started sizing each other up and I guess I'm fresh meat to them.

"Hey!" Emily calls just before she and Marissa switch places.

"Hi," I say back.

Emily positions herself beneath the bar while Marissa resets the weights. I personally don't know how much they can each bench press, but I'm sure it's a lot more than I can do. Not to mention that Emily is literally carrying a one-sided conversation while she does it.

"So...soon..." she says between lifts.

"What is?" I ask.

"The tournament," she huffs before lifting again. "I can't...believe it..."

"Shh," Marissa chides Emily, rolling her eyes. "We try not to encourage her to talk and lift at the same time. It takes too much energy."

"Sorry," I mumble.

"Not...your fault," Emily says with a smile.

"So, like, what are you going to wear?" Marissa asks me. Emily starts to answer, but then Marissa shushes her again and tells her she was asking me.

I stare at her for a second, wondering why she would ask such a strange question. "Aren't we all wearing the same thing? I don't know whether I'm blue or red yet, but..."

"Oh!" Marissa dissolves into a fit of giggles. "I meant to the spring dance. It's the same night and we're all going together. Except, well, Maddy has a date, but we're still kind of going as a group."

"The dance?" If I were still in Hawaii, I totally would have already planned out the entire evening down to the last detail, including who I was going with. But I've been so busy with boxing stuff that I didn't even realize it was the same day as the matches.

"Yeah," Emily says, sitting up on the bench. "We were going to ask if you wanted to join us, but we sorta figured someone would have asked you by now."

"Umm, no, I haven't even been thinking about it," I say to them.

"Really?" Emily says incredulously. "You mean, you don't have a date?"

"No."

"Oh, we just thought…" Emily doesn't finish her sentence.

So Marissa does for her. "We thought since every single guy here has had his eye on you since you moved here, you would have been asked by now."

"What?" I exclaim. Since when have guys been checking me out and how did I not notice? Old Elli would definitely have noticed *that*. What has this country done to me? "I'm sure that's not true."

"It's true," Marissa says with a little laugh. At least she doesn't sound jealous. "But hey, you know, when someone does finally ask you, find out if he has any friends for us. Boys seem to be very intimidated by female boxers."

I look from Emily's friendly smile and inviting hazel eyes to Marissa's shiny blond hair and slim build and wonder what kind of guy would be intimidated by them. I feel like they are so much more deserving of dates for the dance than I am.

"Boys are stupid," I say after a moment. "Especially the ones who don't want to ask you out." I look over to where Denny and Maddy are fighting and with a wry grin, add, "Although, if they've seen you box, maybe there's good reason for them to be afraid."

Emily and Marissa both chuckle and I'm glad I didn't offend them. Emily offers me the bench and I settle onto it while she and Marissa reset the weights—to a substantially lower weight, I might add.

I put my hands on the bar and say, "Would either of you consider throwing a match if I got you a date?"

Emily and Marissa look at each other with matching mischievous faces and then Emily says, "Not a chance, new girl."

*   *   *

I've decided that the spring dance is the perfect place for Julian and Cherry to reconnect. I just have to figure out the logistics of how I'm going to get them both to go together without them knowing it.

I burst into my house, calling for my mom so that I can beg her to take me dress shopping. Mom and I don't always see eye-to-eye on everything, but she has a fantastic sense of style and it's been a long time since we've done anything fun like that together.

"Mom!" I call, going from room to room when she doesn't answer. I find my dad in the living by himself, vacantly staring at the blank TV. "Hey, where's Mom?" I ask him.

He shakes his head. "Mom's not here. She's spending a few days with your Grandma."

"Oh," I say, surprised. "Is everything okay? Is Grandma sick or something?" I don't know my Grandmother that well (beyond her apparent love for knitting me winter hats), but I wouldn't want anything bad to happen to her before I even got a chance to get to know her.

"Grandma's fine," Dad answers in a monotonous voice. "Mom just…" *huge* sigh, "needed a few days away."

My heart drops into my stomach and I swallow audibly. "What—what are you saying?"

"Just that your mom needs a few days away," he says cryptically. Finally he looks up at me and I can see that his eyes are red, like he might have actually been crying, which makes me want to cry.

"Okay," I say softly. "Can I—is there anything you need?"

Dad shakes his head. I start to walk away but then I go back, sit next to him on the couch, and wrap my arms around his neck like I used to do when I was little. He seems surprised, but a split second later, his arms are around me so tightly I almost can't breathe. But I can't pull away. I won't until he does. It doesn't last long, our heartfelt hug, but I think it might have made him feel at least a little better. I give him a small smile and then retreat to my room.

And then I cry because I'm not sure what else to do.

CHAPTER EIGHTEEN

What is happening? Adrian and I are still avoiding each other, Cherry has been giving me the silent treatment for chewing her out, and my *mother* has been gone for three days. I mean, I've talked to her on the phone and I tried to be all normal, and she said she'd go shopping with me this weekend, but like…she hasn't been home.

On top of that, Dan hasn't been seen since Dad dropped that bomb on me, which makes me think his living here had something to do with Mom leaving. And I don't know who to unload on except Julian. But he's starting to get super annoyed that his boxing coach ditched him.

"I'm sorry, Jules. I don't know what to tell you," I say to him. I feel like I've apologized fifty times already, and every time he tells me that it's not my fault and to not worry about it. But I am worried. We still need Dan.

I still need my mom, too.

"Elli," Jules sighs. "For the last time, can you stop trying so hard to be Canadian? Apologies only go so far, and you don't even have anything to apologize for."

"Okay," I say quietly. But I can tell by the way he's beating the crap out of our punching bag that he's really not happy. So I change the subject as I cling a little tighter to the bag to keep it from flying all over the place. "Are you…going to the dance?" I ask.

Julian pauses briefly in his punching but then continues. "Umm, no?"

"Oh."

Punch, punch. "Why do you ask?"

"Doesn't everyone go?" I ask. Why is he still punching the stupid bag? Hasn't he warmed up enough?

"I've never gone to a school dance," he says matter-of-factly.

"What? Julian, what?" I guess I shouldn't be surprised, but I am, and I momentarily let go of the bag.

Which is when Julian decides to throw the hardest punch I've ever seen, effectively knocking the bag straight into my torso. I lose my balance and fall to the floor, howling in a very unladylike fashion.

"I'm so sorry!" Julian practically shouts in my face as he reaches down to help me up.

I put my hand in his and he yanks me upwards a little too fast. With his face inches from my face, he asks, "Are you going?"

Old Elli would probably be swooning at this point. New Elli is wondering why she can't pack on muscle mass like Jules has. "Going…? Oh, to the dance? Yeah, the girls said they would go as a group. You should come, it'll be fun."

Julian stares at me for a second, lets go of my hand, and says, "I'll think about it."

I shake off the weird vibes I just got from Julian and wish for the thousandth time that Dan were here. Without the structure of having our coach dictating our training sessions, we kind of lollygag over what to do after we've warmed up. I want to spar, but Jules sides with Dan on this issue—it's not safe for me, it'll throw him off, yada, yada, excuses.

I sit on the ground with a humph and start stretching out my legs again even though they've already been stretched. "Why are we even doing this if we're not going to spar or receive any training?"

Jules sighs and sits next to me. He can't stretch as far as I can, but he's still pretty limber. "Because I'm supposed to fight a very large and angry person in a month and I'll probably get seriously injured, but I might as well look good while I'm doing it."

"You're going to be just fine," I say with confidence. I really do believe it. He gives me a look. "Red's not really that much bigger than you, you know. In fact, I think you might even be taller than him."

"Well, experience will take care of that for him," he mutters. "You haven't heard from Dan at all?"

I shake my head. Julian, being the amazing friend he is, knew right away that something was wrong when we saw each other the day after my mom left. I told him about it and he was very sympathetic, especially having divorced parents himself. Then when Dan didn't show up for training that night, we assumed the two disappearances were connected.

"What about your mom?" he asks softly.

"We've talked," I told him, trying to sound strong and failing miserably. "Not about… We're going dress shopping tomorrow. For the dance."

Julian nods. "I hope it'll be okay. Do you need, like, a buffer?"

I laugh. "You, buffering between me and my mom while clothes shopping? No offense, but that would be a little weird. Maybe if you were a girl…"

Julian smiles but doesn't say any more. He stops stretching, frowns in thought and then suggests, "We should just watch a movie. What's that one with the boxer?"

"We can't," I say in a scolding voice. "We have too much to do."

Jules just smirks and says, "Consider it research."

Realizing that we're not going to get much done anyway, I cave and find my laptop upstairs. My dad's still in enough of a funk that he doesn't seem to care that I'm down in the basement *with a boy*, of all things.

While we're searching for the movie, I say to Julian, "You know, you're a really good friend." Julian kind of gives me this weird look, so I add quickly, "I didn't mean for that to sound like I was friendzoning you or something. I really do mean it."

Julian surprises me by laughing. "Thanks. I'm not offended. I have a feeling there are many, many guys in your friendzone anyway."

"What do you mean?" I ask.

"Well, you're kind of the play-hard-to-get type, you know?" he says, with an apologetic smile.

I want to refute him, but then I remember how I wouldn't let Adrian kiss me without a literal chase, and how I made Kai follow me around for months before he got up the nerve to almost ask me out. I guess he's right, and I don't know why that bothers me.

"I didn't know…" I mumble without meaning to say it out loud. "Sorry," I say without quite knowing why I'm saying it.

"Oh, don't worry about me, Ella," he says, as he watches the loading screen fill up slowly to 100%. "I mean, yeah, I find you attractive—"

My eyes grow huge and I'm glad it's mostly dark in the basement, but then I start to wonder if he's trying to make a move on me and I think maybe I should turn the lights on.

Then he follows up with, "But you're not…you know…the one."

I stare at him for a second and then burst out laughing. He ducks his head and I can't help but laugh harder, because he's just being so cheesy. But also, it's kind of sweet and I wish briefly for someone who considers me "the one."

"Yeah, yeah, whatever," he says. "Now, shush. I love the opening fanfare."

I clamp my mouth shut and tamp down the urge to laugh more as the movie starts up. It's one of those typical guy movies with a lot of sweat, grunting, and bungled up lines by a guy with a serious slur to his voice. But it's also kind of fun to watch and I recognize pretty much all of the moves they do. I even learn a few things, although I know some of the stuff they do is totally illegal in real tourneys.

Julian leaves shortly after the movie's over and we say goodnight with absolutely no weirdness between us. Honestly, I've never had a guy friend who I didn't feel weird around and it's kind of nice. I hope things never change between us.

*   *   *

Mom and I have been to five stores already and we still can't find the "perfect" dress for the dance. Personally, I'm just too distracted by everything else to think about dresses and dances. Mom's been trying to keep up a conversation with me, but it's all very superficial and I don't trust myself not to yell at her for leaving Dad in the funk that he's in.

Mom finally does notice how very little I've said, and says, "Elli, I know you're probably upset that I left the way I did."

I shrug because public scenes aren't my thing.

She sighs. "Really, it's only meant to be temporary."

"You're coming back?" I say with hope in my voice. Even to my own ears I sound like a little kid, but I don't care. "When?"

"When your uncle leaves," Mom mutters.

"Mom." I touch Mom's arm and make her stop walking right there in the middle of the hallway. It's Saturday and the weather it getting really nice, so it's busy in the mall, but whatever. "Is that why you left?"

"Among other things," she answers.

I don't even bother with the other things. "Mom, Uncle Dan hasn't been seen since you left. You can come back. Please?"

"Really?" Mom asks in a strange voice. I nod vigorously. "Your father never told me."

"Probably because you made him choose between his wife and his brother," I blurt out. I regret the comment immediately and slap a hand over my mouth. Even if it were true—which I don't know if it is—I should *never* have said something like that. Ugh, that's why I didn't want to bring it up while shopping, of all things.

Mom gives me a hurt look and then starts walking away. I don't know where she's going or if she intends to just leave me at the mall, but I race after her.

"Mom, I'm sorry," I say. "I shouldn't have—"

"No, you shouldn't have," she says tightly without looking at me.

"Look, Mom, Dan is gone," I tell her. "He hasn't even shown up to train me and Julian. Just come home and talk to Dad. Please? He's seriously depressed."

"And what about my feelings, Elli?" she asks, he anger fading to sadness. "Why should I consider his if he never considers mine?"

I don't know what to say. I stopped paying attention to my parents' arguments years ago because I figured they had nothing to do with me. It was just kind of this normal thing where they'd fight and then pretend it never happened in front of me. But now it's real, and it matters to me; it always mattered to them and I feel selfish for never bothering to care about it before now.

But that was the old Elli. The new Elli is a fighter. And if my parents won't fight for each other, for their marriage, then I guess I'll have to do it for them.

"Please, Mom," I say once more. "There must be something…"

Mom just shakes her head.

"Look, just come over for lunch or something tomorrow. I'll make you lunch. Or dinner. Or even dessert if you just want dessert and we can all sit down together."

I'm trying too hard. She totally knows it, too. Which is probably why she agrees. Now all I have to do is find a recipe for tiramisu and a reason to ditch them tomorrow night.

Mom shuts down that conversation pretty quickly and we get back into an almost-comfortable rhythm of shopping. I try on, like, a hundred dresses or something like that until Mom throws a seemingly ordinary one over the dressing room door.

"Coral blue?" I say with disappointment rising up in my throat. I used to *love* wearing coral blue until I was about thirteen and this girl in my class told me that it washed out my face. I know it sounds stupid, but that was a pretty traumatic experience for me. I mean, I threw out everything I owned that was that colour and I never looked back.

"Come on, Elli, you love that colour," Mom reminds me. It's true, I still do love it. "Just try it."

"Okay…" I say hesitantly. I close my eyes, slip the dress on, and then leave the dressing room without even peeking. "How bad is it?"

"Oh, sweetie," Mom says in a gooey voice that she rarely ever uses. "You're beautiful. Would you open your eyes and look in the mirror? That Julian doesn't stand a chance."

"Mom, you remembered his name," I say, opening my eyes to look at her. "Also, there's nothing going on—"

Suddenly, I can't speak because I look at the mirror and I have to admit that she's right. I do look kind of beautiful in the dress that totally does not wash out my colouring at all. Maybe there's something in the air in Canada, or maybe Canadian coral blue is different or something, but the dress is amazing. This changes everything.

I check out the price tag. The dress is on sale. Obviously, this was meant to be.

Mom buys me the dress even though I insisted that it was within my budget. I keep trying to get her to not pay for it, but she tells me that she's proud of me and wants to do this. And maybe she's trying to buy my love or something, but those words mean so much more to me than money or some dress.

When Mom drops me off at home, I make her promise that she really is coming for dessert tomorrow. She does—no less than five times—and finally kicks me out of her car with a teasing smile and a pat on my cheek. I give her a kiss and skip inside.

CHAPTER NINETEEN

I made the tiramisu but didn't stick around to find out whether it was even good or not. I opted instead to go running before my mom showed up. I mean, I should be running a lot more than I do anyway, so I figured it was a good excuse. Of course, I probably should have warned Dad that Mom was coming over but it umm…slipped my mind?

Judging by the amount of missing tiramisu and the two dirty dishes I find in the sink later, neither of them minded too much.

I want to be happy about that, but I literally haven't seen my uncle in two weeks. We're two weeks away from competition. I have my girls to back me up, but Julian is starting to freak out and I don't know how to help him. Not to mention the girls are starting to get into competitive mode, so they aren't *too* willing to give all their secrets away.

I've tried asking my dad where Dan might be, but he just says that Dan's working and that he's found his own place which is why he hasn't been around. I've tried patiently explaining that that's not a very good excuse for ditching his trainees, but Dad doesn't have much of an answer for that.

I wish I could complain to Mom about it, but I don't want to stoke the flames. Plus she hasn't really been around a lot either. I mean, I talk to her on the phone, and I've visited with her and Grandma (who gave me *another* knitted hat even though it's May), and she's even come home a few times. But it's still kind of tense around here.

I can't complain to Julian about it because I'm too busy listening to *him* complaining and freaking out, and Cherry's still not really happy with me. Which leaves…

Adrian. I stare at his number in my phone for a million years before I finally press the call button. It rings twice before he answers.

"Hi!" he sounds surprised, happy, and a little uncertain.

I feel kind of bad for bothering him, especially after the way I've treated him. And I'm not sure how to say it or anything I'm feeling so I say instead, "Want to go for a run with me?"

There's a pause on his end. Did he hear me? "Right now?" Oh—he did.

"Never mind," I say, feeling stupid. "I shouldn't have bothered you. I'm sorry."

"Elli, wait," he says quickly. "There's a park down the street from school. Do you know how to get there?"

"Yes," I say eagerly.

"Meet me there," he says.

I agree and then we hang up without belabouring the point. You know those couples who are always like "*You* hang up first," "No, *you*," even though it's super annoying to everyone else around them? Yeah, that's definitely not us.

Mostly because we're not a couple.

But if we were, that wouldn't be us.

I put my running clothes on and tell Dad I'm going out. He replies by sarcastically asking if he should be expecting a visit from my mom. I say,

"You never know," and leave before he can ask more questions.

I have to admit that it's gotten really nice outside. The air is warm and holds fragrant scents from the early-spring flowers blooming in people's gardens. If I don't think too much, if I don't focus too hard on the minute details, I almost feel like I'm back in Hawaii. If I turn left twice, run about a mile, take a right, and then run to the end of the road, I'll end up at the beach where my friends are waiting in beachwear. Kai will be there, all happy and smiling, with a surfboard in his hands, waiting to impress me with his moves.

Reality takes me back to where I am, the park by the high school in Canada, where just weeks before, children were still making snow angels. Now, they're dousing themselves on a splash pad (even though it's not *that* nice out), the grass has grown green again, and a dark-haired boy with chocolate eyes is chilling on a bench acting like he totally doesn't see me jogging up to him.

"Try keeping up, Ontario," I call to him as I rush past his bench. I watch Adrian bolt off of the bench, wondering if the nickname I just gave him sounds as cute as "Hawaii," or if it sounds as stupid as I think it does.

"You run like a girl, Hawaii," he says as he catches up to me.

"I *am* a girl," I inform him. "In case you haven't noticed."

"Oh, I noticed," he says, giving my entire body a brief once-over.

Heat floods my cheeks and I'm hoping he either won't notice or will think it's just from the exertion of running. We both decide to shut up and our steps fall in sync as our shoes slap the pavement. I sneak glances at Adrian and all thoughts of Hawaii leave my mind. He seems so at ease, like running is just a thing he does, the same as breathing or blinking. I wonder if it could be like that for me if I kept up with it. Maybe I will keep running. Maybe I'll even keep boxing.

We run for what feels like a really long time and even though I'm tired and my body hurts, I don't want to stop. I know when I stop, I'll have to say things—explain—things, and I'm not quite ready.

Adrian is actually the one that stops us. He barely looks winded, but he leads me to a bench, saying how I've pushed myself hard enough for today. I don't know how he can tell that I was just at my breaking point, but I'm kind of glad he called it.

We sit and after a moment, Adrian asks, "Still missing Hawaii?"

I nod and he looks a little disappointed. "I grew up there," I tell him so he won't take it so personally. "It's still…home to me."

Okay, so judging by the look on his face, that just made it worse.

"It's not so bad here, though," I add. I look at the quaint little neighbourhood where we've stopped. It's all century homes with wrought iron fences and elaborate front gardens. I kind of like how old it feels. There aren't many places like this in Hawaii. "I mean, once you get past winter, that is."

Adrian laughs and *oh, gosh*, his dimples. "I guess you miss your friends and…stuff."

"Stuff?" I laugh. "Friends and stuff?"

"Yeah. I thought maybe you had, like, a boyfriend that you're keeping up with long distance," he says, acting all shy suddenly. "I mean, I don't want to be presumptuous, but I never really asked. I don't want to get in the way of that."

I smile at him, because I can't help myself. I almost mention Kai, but instead I say, "I don't have a boyfriend in Hawaii. Or…anywhere, actually."

He nods, a perplexed little frown wrinkling his forehead. Then he gives me this look that melts my insides right before he leans in and kisses me. I can't tell whether the kiss lasts forever or for only a split second, because it feels like both, but when it ends I smile really big at Adrian. Which makes him smile, which melts me inside out all over again.

"That was nice," I say, which is quite possibly the lamest thing anyone could say after a kiss like that.

Adrian's eyes crinkle in a smile, and he asks, "Is that why you called me today?"

My eyes grow wide. Why *did* I call him? Oh yeah... "Oh, no. I'm just...really on edge. I didn't know who to talk to."

He turns on the bench so that he's fully facing me and says, "Okay, so talk to me."

And then it all comes spilling out. How my mom left the day my uncle ditched us, and I don't know if either I or Julian will be able to compete properly. How things are so much worse between my parents than I originally thought. How Cherry is mad at me, even though she has no real reason to be. That I think she just needs to work things out with Julian, and my plan to get them back together.

I even tell him about my uncle's alcoholism, because I'm worried that something went wrong and that he might have gone back to it and I have no idea how to find out. I finish by saying that I wish I'd never dragged Julian into a fight he doesn't need or deserve and how it was a poor decision to involve my unreliable uncle.

He listens to all of it intently, giving little sounds of encouragement. At times I wonder if I'm speaking too fast, but he never looks away and his eyes don't even glaze over. As I get to the part about my parents, he even takes my hands and squeezes them. When I'm finished, I sit back to let it sink in.

Finally, he says, "I can see now why you miss Hawaii. Seems much less complicated there."

I laugh a little. I like that he's trying to make me feel better. "Less complicated, but also less..."

"Less what?" he asks patiently.

I shrug. "I don't know. I feel like a completely different person than the sulky girl I was when we left Hawaii. I left a life of blissful ignorance behind, but I feel...stronger here. More like the real me."

He gives me a half smile. "Aw, so it's not all that bad then?"

I shake my head. "But now things are kind of messed up."

Adrian's still holding my hands and he squeezes them again. "Well, I don't know what to tell you about all that. But maybe I can help a little?"

"Really?" I ask hopefully. I want to suggest that maybe he should just kiss me again until the tournament is over, but I don't think that's physically possible.

"Well, for starters, Julian needs some serious help still, it seems," he says, completely ignorant of my internal ramblings. "Some of my friends have been on the boxing team before, so I'll talk to them. See if they can practice with Julian as much as possible before the tourney."

"You'd really do that? Oh, Adrian, that would be great!" I reach forward and hug him, which earns me yet another beautiful smile. I don't think I'll ever get tired of his smiles.

"No problem," he replies. "I don't know what to tell you about Cherry, though. I do not understand how friendships between girls work at all. Sorry."

"That's okay," I say. "I think I can figure that out on my own."

He nods. "About your parents though... I know it's hard, but try not to get too involved."

I give him this look like he's crazy, but also like I'm curious as to why he would give me that piece of information.

"Trust me," he says. "My parents have been separated for two years. They're not divorced and they're not with other people. But they're also not with each other. I don't know—it's kind of weird. All I know is they make their own decisions regardless of what my brother and I do and say, and sometimes trying to help makes things worse."

"Okay, I can take that," I tell him. He's right about one thing: that's hard to hear. Maybe he's right about the rest, too. "I guess that probably goes for Uncle Dan, too."

"Probably," he agrees. "I mean, that's his business. I know it affects you, but what can you do? In the meantime, like I said, I'll see if we can help Julian out. I can't think of a single person who doesn't want to see Julian win."

"Except Red, you mean," I mutter.

Adrian chuckles. "I think even Red wants to see Julian put up a good fight."

"Before he beats him senseless?" I say wryly. I don't really mean it, but I guess a tiny part of me is afraid of the possibility.

"Don't worry, it won't happen," he promises. "Not if I have anything to say about it. Do you want to go to the dance with me?"

What a segue.

"Umm, I kind of already told the girls we'd go in a group," I say, my voice laced with regret.

"Oh," he says, clearly disappointed.

"But…I could probably change my mind if they all had dates," I say, raising my eyebrows suggestively.

Adrian sighs exaggeratedly. "Now I have to match-make just to get a date with you?" I nod my head vigorously, giving him my most winning smile. He laughs. "Okay, okay, I'll see what I can do."

"Thanks, Adrian," I say meaningfully. "I really do appreciate it. All of it."

Adrian walks me home after that. I realize that throughout our conversation, I didn't even learn anything about him, except that he's a huge sweetheart. So I ask him a load of questions, all of which he answers surprisingly openly.

Adrian's lived in the same house his whole life. He lives with his Dad—his mom rents the house next door. They are separate, but not really because she shares at least three dinners a week with them and they still pay their bills together. He has a St Bernard named Sugar. His favourite hot drink is a chai tea, but he doesn't want me to tell anyone because it's not very manly to like chai tea.

He likes playing hockey, but he *loves* playing piano. I'm also not allowed to tell anyone that. I promise not to if he promises to play for me sometime. He agrees, and then we're at my house and I'm a little sad that our pseudo-date is over.

"See you, Elli," he says with a wink.

I lick my lips but I don't get another kiss. Oh well, there's always the dance.

CHAPTER TWENTY

One week until the competition and I still haven't heard from Dan. I've called him a million times; I even asked my dad to call him. At this point, I'm desperate enough to hope that he left the GPS on his phone on. That's how I found him last time. I never wanted to track him down like that again, but desperate times call for desperate measures, I guess.

I turn my phone's GPS on and some dots pop up on the map, indicating where some of my contacts are. To be perfectly honest, I think it's a little creepy that I can find my contacts like this, which is why I didn't want to have to use it. But like I said, I'm getting a little desperate. I'm also more than a little furious, but I'm trying to keep my priorities straight.

I can't believe it—one of the dots belongs to my uncle. He actually left his phone's location on. Good. Serves him right for just ditching me and Julian. I put on my running/training clothes and start following the map on my phone.

I think about asking someone to go with me, but I'm not sure who to ask. I want to ask Adrian, but although he's been very sweet to me over the past week, I've already asked him for too much. Not only did he enlist *several* of his friends to help get Julian some last-minute training, but he also went out of his way to find out which ones are going solo to the dance.

This part of town is starting to look sketchy, and I'm a little afraid of where my phone is leading me. In a few minutes, I realize why: my uncle is at a bar. A part of me wants to believe that I'm mistaken, that maybe he's not in there getting drunk or already drunk. But I know my hopes are farfetched.

I stand outside a bar called Shots, close enough that the bouncer starts to give me a funny look. I know I can't go inside, and I really don't want to, but I also want to find my uncle and tell him how furious I am at him right now.

Finally, when I've been standing there long enough, the bouncer says, "Hey kid, little young to be here, aren't you?"

"Yes," I answer simply, still staring at the neon sign indicating the bar's name. I look at the bouncer and say, "I'm trying to find my uncle. He's a recovering alcoholic. Or at least…he's supposed to be recovering."

The bouncer snorts, which feels a little offensive to me for some reason, and juts his thumb toward the entrance. "Got plenty of them in here."

"Wonderful," I mutter.

The bouncer gives me a sympathetic look and then surprises me by saying, "Maybe I can find him for you. You got a picture of him?"

"Really? Yeah, here." I pull up Dan's contact picture on my cell phone and show it to the guy.

He makes me promise to wait outside—which I do—and then goes inside. He comes out a few minutes later, dragging my uncle behind him who is swearing up and down that he's not drunk.

"Ssseriousssly, guy," Dan slurs, his eyes half-lidded, his face red. "I'm not drunk that much…"

"Yeah, you've had enough," the bouncer tells him, not unkindly, before pushing him in my direction.

Dan bumps into me, starts to apologize, and then realizes who I am. "Elli!" His eyes open a bit in surprise and I can tell he's trying to act more sober than he is. "What are you doing here?"

I stare at him hard, shaking my head. "You *promised*. You promised you wouldn't drink. You promised you'd be there for me and Julian."

"Elli, I—"

"I don't even want to hear it, Uncle Dan." It's totally rude to cut someone off like that, but then again, he deserves it.

I start to walk away from him and he stumbles after me, but nearly trips over his own feet. I can't help it—I reach out to stop him from falling. Catching a grown man who's drunk is not easy, but we manage to stay upright. I sigh, knowing I can't just leave him like that.

I ask him for his phone, which he gives me without much of a fight. I think he's too drunk to realize that I intend to call his Get Dry sponsor. Recalling her name—Liz—I look her up in his contacts and hope that she'll answer.

"Hello?" she sounds groggy, like I woke her, and I feel a little bad. But it's not even that late, and I hope she'll understand that I need her.

"Hi, Liz?" I say uncertainly.

"Not her," Dan whines.

"Yes..." There's that wispy voice again. When I hear a voice like that, it makes me think the person I'm talking to is made out of thin air.

"Hi, my name is Elli. We met once? I'm—"

"Dan's niece," she says quickly. "The boxer. I remember."

Well, I'm not really a boxer, but I don't correct her. "Look, I hate to call you like this, but Dan is...well, he's drunk."

"Mnot drunk," Dan says loudly, trying to get close to the phone.

"He's not exactly making his case," Liz says, sounding annoyed. "I'm assuming he's at Shots again?"

Again? "Yeah," I answer. "Has he been here a lot lately?"

"Yes," she says with a wafer-thin sigh. "And he won't tell me why."

There's a pause of expectation and I know she's waiting to see if I'll tell her anything. "Sorry, but I wish I knew myself," I tell her, eyeing Dan. "It might have something to do with my parents, but Dan hasn't spoken to me since he moved out of our house."

"Sshhh," Dan whispers noisily. "Don't tell her that."

"Oh, well that's good to know," she says, sounding totally ticked off. "Can you hang out for a few minutes with him? I'll be there soon."

"Sure," I say. What else am I supposed to do? I tap off and as I hand Dan his phone back, I say, "Liz is coming."

"Aw, Elli, why'd you do that?" Dan asks, ripping the phone from my fingers.

"Because you're a drunk," I saw unapologetically, staring him straight in the eye.

Dan glowers at me then stares at the pavement. He clumsily shoves the phone into his pocket and says, "You don't know what it's like, Elli. You don't just one day decide you don't want to be an alcoholic and never drink again. It's not that simple."

"Yeah, I get it," I snap at him. "But you're supposed to wean off it. Not get drunk over and over again."

"You can't just completely cut it out—"

"Well, you can't just completely cut people out of your life either!" I finally look at him. I'm aware of the bouncer, watching our interaction, probably just on the verge of stepping in if we get too into our argument. I also realize that people are coming and going around the bar's entrance, so I try to lower my voice and not make a scene. "You let me down, Uncle Dan."

He sighs wearily. "I know. I'm not perfect, okay?"

I blink back the tears burning at the back of my eyes. "I know you're not."

"But you wanted me to be," he cuts in, looking straight into my eyes. His are a little red, but he seems a whole lot more sober than he was a minute ago. "You had this grand idea that I'd make Julian a world-class fighter in only three months. Three months! What were you thinking?"

I bite back a scathing retort. "I was thinking that maybe it would distract you. That you'd realize there's more to live for."

"That's a little ambitious, don't you think?" he asks. He's not joking. I just shrug. "Okay, I get it. I let you down. I let Julian down. I came onto your mom and now everyone hates me—you, Julian, Shauna, Rob...Liz. That is why I'm here. That's why I'm drinking."

My eyes open wide and I can barely look my uncle in the eye. "You did what to my mom?"

He frowns and says, "You didn't know?"

"No!" I see a car coming up in the distance and I wonder if it's Liz. "Mom just up and went to stay with Grandma."

"I...I didn't know," he says. He's looking at the car that's slowly creeping to a stop near us.

"That's..." I sigh. "Why?" I know he had a thing for her once upon a time, but he said he was over that.

"Sometimes...you just never get over a person," he admits and it seems like the admission takes all his energy because he's suddenly droopy and no longer angry. "You know? You just like them so much, but you don't want to, and you hate yourself for still feeling that way, which makes you resent them even though you still want them. It's complicated. And I know it was wrong, so I don't need a little lecture from you."

"I wasn't going to lecture you," I say. And I mean it. What would I even say to him? I have to admit that it's true that I don't fully understand everything he's going through. I glance over to the car where Liz is getting out of the driver's side.

"I'm sorry if I've been hard on you," I say softly to him.

Dan gives me a look I can't quite interpret until he says, "I wish I had more Ellis in my life."

And that's when I realize the look he gave me is appreciation, which makes me feel kind of good.

Liz stalks up to Dan and slaps him soundly. "Daniel Smith, how dare you leave me hanging for weeks? How dare you let your niece find you like this?"

My eyes are probably the size of saucers. Liz still has that wispy thin voice, but her tone is so no-nonsense it's not even funny. And I would not have wanted to be on the receiving end of that slap. Can sponsors even do that?

"Liz, I'm sorry," he says, and by the tone of his voice, I can tell he really is sorry that Liz is mad at him.

"Oh, you haven't even begun to understand how sorry you're gonna be," she tells him sternly.

Strangely enough, Dan just smiles at Liz, and I can see that it's her undoing. She can't help smiling back and I know there's definitely something more going on between them than just a sponsor relationship. I clear my throat to remind them of my presence and quickly get their attention.

Liz's smile disappears. "I'm taking you both home."

"I don't have a home," Dan mutters darkly, making me wonder where he's been the last few weeks.

"Just come home with me," I tell him, extending an olive branch. We get into Liz's car and I remind him, "Mom's not even home anyway."

After a few minutes of quiet driving, Dan says quietly, "Your dad hates me."

I reach forward and put my hand on his shoulder. "I'm sure he doesn't hate you. He's your brother," I say gently.

"I don't want him to see me like this," he complains.

"Too bad," Liz says, turning down a familiar street. "If I take you back to the hotel, I know you'll just get drunker."

Dan just slouches down into his seat in response. He sulks silently for the rest of the ride while I think about how he's been staying in a hotel getting drunk. I hope what Liz said was an exaggeration, but now I'm not so sure. It occurs to me that I don't really know my uncle as well as I thought I did. I decide at that moment that I will change that. Starting tonight, even.

*   *   *

The Plan

Step 1: I've already invited Mom and Dad to come watch my fight. I know I won't do well, but they'll be proud of me and they'll have something to do together. They'll have to figure out the rest of their own.

Step 2: I'm hoping my uncle will come to the fight too, even if he's done with coaching us. To be honest, there's not much time left for coaching anyway, if it would even do any good. However, I'm still optimistic that there can be a happily ever after for my family, no matter how messed up things are right now.

Step 3: The dance. I mean, I've already technically got a date and a group of friends to go with, but this isn't about me. It's about Julian and Cherry. Julian has tentatively agreed to go. Cherry is another issue—I know it'll be like pulling teeth to get her to go, but if I can do it, then there may still be some hope for her and Jules.

Step 4: More kisses from Adrian. Lots more kisses.

CHAPTER TWENTY-ONE

I can tell Julian is wigging out with it being so close to the tournament. I couldn't find him in the cafeteria at lunch today—there's just a group of kids hanging out at our table, presumably waiting for him. So I've gone to the library to check if he's here instead. I figure a nerdy kid like him would take comfort among the stacks.

And of course I found him here, in the sci-fi section, reading a thick book that features a warrior-looking guy on a horse with a long, majestic sword. Julian's sitting on the floor, pretending he hasn't noticed that I'm here, so I plop down next to him.

I let him read a minute longer—maybe he has a really long sentence to finish, who knows?—and then I ask, "Are you nervous?"

"That's an understatement," he answers without looking up.

I put my hand over the book, about to give him the pep talk of the century but what comes out is, "What are you reading?"

"It's from a series called *The Wheel of Time*. It's about...well, a lot of stuff happens." He shuts the book so I can see the cover more clearly and says, "This was my favourite series when I was younger. I was just trying to distract myself for a bit."

"Is it working?" I ask gently.

"No."

"Jules, you're gonna be fine," I tell him. But my voice sounds scared even to myself.

"I'm going to lose, Ella," he says, not quite able to meet my eyes. "Even with Dan and everyone else helping me over the next few days, I know I won't even last one round. I don't know why I ever thought I could do this."

"Because you *can*." This time I sound convincing. I think. "Really, I know you can. You've come so far. You're amazing. Everyone believes in you. Did you say Dan is helping you?"

He nods with a frown. "Didn't you know? I assumed that was your doing…"

I shake my head. "I talked to him a couple of nights ago, but he was drunk, and he didn't mention it."

Julian looks at his watch. "It's almost time for math. I'm failing."

"What?" I practically shout, having forgotten that I'm sitting in the library.

Julian stands up and reaches a hand down for me. "Well, okay, I'm getting a seventy-five, but still. I've never gotten lower than eighty-two in anything."

I start to laugh, but then stop at the death glare he gives me. "Sorry, for a second I thought you were joking."

"It's not a joke," he says, sounding irritated. "I haven't had time for homework because of this tournament that I don't even want to do. And it makes me look stupid. It makes me feel stupid."

"Julian, you're not—"

"I can't box and I don't have good grades, so where does that leave me?" he continues. He's not even looking at me. "Nowhere. That's where it leaves me."

I'm not sure what to say so I just follow him out of the library. He gives me a weird look which I return with a frown.

Then he says, "You don't have to follow me, Elli."

"I'm not following you," I say indignantly. "We have math together."

"Oh, yeah," he mumbles.

I pull on his arm to stop him before he goes into the classroom. "Julian, there's still time to pick up your grades." I meant to say something encouraging about the tournament but that's all I could come up with.

"I know that," he snaps and I wonder why he seems so mad at me.

All throughout math class I stare at the back of Julian's head (because he insists on sitting in the front row and I'm not in a front row kind of mood). I'm trying to understand why he's so upset with *me*, in particular, when it hits me. Earlier he said "this tournament that I don't even want to do." Meaning, he's still only doing it for me. But is he really still holding a grudge over that? And why? He could have dropped out of the tournament at any point. I never forced him to exercise or train, and I never made him have his parents sign the paperwork.

The longer I sit in class behind his stupid head, the angrier I get that he's angry at me. Finally, in the middle of the teacher's lesson, I stick up my hand, tell him I'm not feeling well, and gather my things and leave. I don't look back to see if Julian's looking or not, but I don't care.

I stalk down the halls until I make it to the back doors that lead to the football field. There's a group of guys in football gear stretching on the ground, running laps, and pushing blocking dummies across the field. And of course I see Adrian—who I guess needs something to do now that hockey is over—doing a warm-up jog. He alters his course so that he's running straight towards me. How does he always seem to know when I'm around?

"Hawaii," he says in greeting with a little half grin. "Big day's coming up."

"Yeah," I answer.

"What's wrong?" he asks, his eyebrows lowered in concern.

"Julian's all mad at me because it's my fault he joined the tournament," I blurt out. "It's like I forced him into it. And I guess I forced all those people to help him out and be nice to him and want to hang out with him and make him super popular. Is that what he thinks? Because, if so, then I'm *so* sorry that people think he's cool."

"Is that really why he's mad?" Adrian asks sceptically.

I shrug, not really able to look Adrian in the eye. "He thinks he's going to lose badly and maybe he thinks everyone will treat him differently afterwards."

"Maybe he thinks *you'll* treat him differently afterwards," Adrian suggests softly.

"What?" I say, finally looking up at him.

Adrian hesitates. "Maybe he's afraid of being a failure in your eyes. Not theirs."

"I don't think he's a failure," I say firmly.

"We all know that," Adrian says, and I can tell he's trying to be patient with me. "All you ever say is how good Julian is at boxing, how great he's going to do at the tournament. But what if he doesn't? What if he gets knocked out in the first round?"

"He won't—"

"But what if he does?" Adrian persists. "Will you think any differently of him? Would you still be so supportive?"

"Obviously," I say. But I see Adrian's point. I begrudgingly nod my head. "Okay, I get what you're saying. But what do you expect me to do? Tell him he'll never make it but it's okay because I'm still his friend?"

Adrian sighs. "No…not like that. But you could put a little less pressure on him."

"I didn't realize I was pressuring him," I say in a small voice. Maybe Adrian's right, though. Maybe Julian feels like I've put too much on him.

"Well…"

"Okay, I get it," I say, giving his shoulder a little push. "Geez, when did you become so touchy-feely?"

Adrian smirks, and I can tell he feels like he won something. "Don't tell anyone. I have a reputation to keep."

I don't want Adrian to think he has total control in this conversation, so I put my hands around his head, pull him in for a quick kiss and then say, "Your secret's safe with me."

The wide-eyed look on his face as I wave goodbye is totally worth it.

*   *   *

Three days until the tournament. That's all that's left. Julian and I are in my basement with Dan, trying to cram in as much last-minute training as we can without hurting ourselves. I haven't had a chance yet to really talk to Julian, to apologize or try to smooth things over. After I left math today, we didn't see each other, and since he got to my house we've just been in go mode.

Dan is watching me doing forms, picking apart every single movement I'm making. I'm trying not to sigh every single time he barks out an order or tells me to "do it again with feeling," but it's getting increasingly difficult. I meet Julian's eyes and he gives me a sympathetic look which makes me feel a little better.

My uncle's cell phone starts ringing and I stop moving and give him a hopeful look. Maybe he'll let me take a little break…

Dan rolls his eyes and then takes his phone out of his pocket. "Okay, have a break while I take this." He waves his hand impatiently as he walks away from us.

Julian comes over to me as I try to fix the tape on my hands. I can't quite meet his eyes and I'm not sure what to say to him.

"You're too tense, Ella," he says gently. He takes my hands and adjusts the tape for me. "You need to loosen up a bit."

I look up at him, surprised that he's trying to help me. "I'm sorry," I say.

"Don't be sorry to me," he says. "I just don't want you to freeze up in the ring. You can hurt yourself."

"Not for that," I say. I'm caught off guard by how nice he's being, but it makes apologizing easier. "I'm sorry that I got you into this mess. And that I haven't been…as supportive as I should have been."

Jules raises an eyebrow at me. "What are you talking about? You've been nothing but supportive."

"I just mean…" How do I say this without sounding like a jerk? "I want you to know that even if you don't beat Red—which I totally think you could—I'll still be here for you. You know? You've been my friend since the first day you met me and I want to be just as good a friend to you."

Jules scrunches up his eyebrows and just stares at me for a minute. Then his face breaks out into a grin. "Ella, I think we both know that I'm not going to win. But thank you. I really appreciate it."

I smile. "You could do it, you know. I still believe in you."

"Thanks." He hesitates a moment and then says, "I'm sorry, too. For snapping at you today. You didn't deserve that."

"Maybe I did," I say with a shrug.

"You're my best friend," he says meaningfully. "I never want to treat you like that."

His comment makes me feel all warm and fuzzy inside. I want to say something nice back, but I don't get a chance because Dan comes back with a scowl on his face and claps his hands twice, which is my cue to retake my stance and continue doing my forms.

*   *   *

I leave our training session early because tonight I have to go to the rink to help set up for the Home Show that's going on this weekend. Cherry's parents know that I can't be here on Saturday to help out because of the tournament, but they do need a lot of help to get the place ready to open tomorrow. Apparently the Home Show is a big deal for the home reno companies that showcase their services throughout the weekend.

I'm duct taping some cords down to the floor when I hear an annoyed voice above me ask, "What are you doing here?"

I don't need to see the star-studded black rain boots to know that Cherry is standing over me, probably giving me a disapproving look.

"What does it look like?" I say, immediately regretting mirroring her tone of voice.

"It looks like you're not getting ready for your tournament," she says as she lowers herself to the ground. She wordlessly picks up the duct tape and helps me finish taping down my section of the cords.

"I still have a job," I say to her.

"You should be training," Cherry says emphatically. She stands up with me. "I'll go see if you can leave early."

She almost starts walking away, but I grab her arm first. "Cherry, don't worry. I already did my training after school today. It's okay. Besides—I'm not the one who has to fight Red, remember?"

"Still…" Cherry actually sounds like she feels bad that I'm there.

"It's okay, really." I smile at her to show that I'm not as cranky as I first sounded. "What are you doing here?"

"It's the Home Show," she says matter-of-factly, leading me to the next section that needs taping. "My parents always freak out because it's their biggest money-maker for spring and if I don't help out then I'll never hear the end of it."

"Does that mean you'll miss the fight on Saturday?" I ask. It hadn't occurred to me that Cherry wouldn't be going, but now that I'm thinking about it, I wonder if she had ever planned to go.

Cherry just shrugs and starts ripping off long lengths of duct tape. I help her for a few minutes, waiting for her to elaborate, but she never does.

"I know you don't like the idea," I say gently, "but I think Julian would really like it if you were there."

"Why? So he can show off his masculine prowess to me?" she blurts, punctuating her rhetorical question by rapidly ripping off some duct tape.

"No," I answer. "So that he can have people who care about him there to support him. No matter what happens."

Cherry's eyes widen slightly. "You don't think he can win?"

I smile a little, thinking about how well Julian boxes compared to me. But I know, having never seen him in the ring, it's anyone's bet. "I think Julian can do anything he sets his mind to. But just because he loses a match doesn't mean he has to lose his friends, right?"

"I guess you're right," she agrees and I almost want to cheer. But I don't, because that would be weird, and it might also make her change her mind.

But there's one more thing I have to push for. "We're going to the dance after, too."

"Together?" she asks a little too loudly, and I know I've got her.

I smile on the inside, but outwardly I laughed airily. "Not like that. As a group. Me and the girls, and him and…Adrian's going, too."

Cherry rolls her eyes and then grins at me. "Oh, Elli. You really think the whole school doesn't see how gaga you two are over each other?"

I cringe. "Is it that obvious?"

Cherry laughs, which is all the answer I really need. "Look, thanks for the invite, but—"

I have to think of something quickly before she says no, so I blurt out, "Julian really wants you to go but doesn't think you'd say yes if he asked."

I can't even pretend that's not a lie. It is. You know it is because Julian himself hasn't even said for sure that he's going.

"Really?" Cherry asks softly, insecurely.

"I wasn't supposed to say that." That, at least, is the truth. "But yes. Come on, it'll be fun. And I promise not to do anything stupid with you guys."

"Oh, well..." I hold my breath and wait for the answer, which is a satisfying, "Okay, fine."

"Yay!" I proclaim, making Cherry look around us subconsciously. I grab her hands and say, "It's going to be so much fun."

"Yeah, yeah," she says, pulling her hands away. "Now back to work, or I'm sending you home to do more...whatever it is you boxers do."

I laugh. Everything is falling into place nicely. Now all I have to do is not get knocked out in the first round on Saturday.

CHAPTER TWENTY-TWO

I'm not shaking because I'm nervous for my match, or because my parents are sitting in the stands, or because the girls insist that we don't talk to each other on tournament day, or because I'm not actually that good at boxing, or even because I know that my parents are going to take me out to dinner and Dan will be there too and it'll be awkward.

No, I'm nervous because Julian and Red's fight is a mere 20 minutes away. And I can't even stay with him because the boys and girls are in their own separate locker rooms. I'll only be able to go out to watch him fight, but I've already chewed off all of my nails and have none left for when I'm watching.

I'm rubbing my forehead pretty vigorously when Emily breaks the code to say to me, "Relax, Elli. Tensing up will only make you feel worse."

I look into her kind eyes. I appreciate her words, but they won't do a thing for Julian. "It's not me I'm worried about," I say quietly, while the other girls give us warning looks.

Emily gives me an understanding smile and nods, but doesn't say anything else. I'm not sure what to do with myself, so I take my cue from the others and sit on the ground to do some stretches. I have to say though, we all look pretty cute in our boxing gear. Underneath the little boxing shorts and short tank tops, we're all wearing these weird chest protectors. It's like, a bra times a thousand, and it's weird but totally necessary.

One of the female gym teachers—whose name I don't know, because I'm not actually in gym class—comes in to tell us there's five minutes until the fight and that we can go out if we want to watch. Of course we all go out and discover that almost everyone in the upper grades has come to watch. The school must have made some good money off selling all those tickets.

Red and Julian haven't been announced yet, so they're not in the ring. Dan is standing in one corner, so I go up to the ring and ask the ref—who turns out to be our librarian, Mr. Pfizer—if it's okay to stay on that side. It's a little unconventional, but since Dan is my trainer too, Mr. Pfizer allows it.

"Are you nervous?" I ask my uncle.

He turns to me and after a moment's pause, says, "He'll be fine."

I smile at Dan and am rewarded with the first smile he's given me since before I found him drunk at that bar. Dan is a tough coach, but I don't think Julian and I would have learned to box any other way. He kept us motivated, pushed us to our limits, and made us do the hard stuff. And I'm really grateful for that now.

As we wait for Julian and Red to come out, Dan tells me how they have both already defeated two other boxers and that this is the last match for the boys today. When he tells me about how well Julian did, I feel pride swelling inside me, but I'm also a little disappointed that I missed those two matches. At least we were allowed to come out for this one. I think the teachers knew that no one would want to miss it.

Finally, Julian and Red are announced and they both step up into the ring. I feel a little bad that everyone boos when Red is announced, until he steps up into the ring and raises a middle finger in the air. Then I join in with the booing. I wonder if Red is annoyed that he got stuck on the blue side, while Julian is wearing the red gear, and I have to stifle a giggle.

Julian, on the other hand, earns some ear-shattering screams when he walks out. I study his face while he and Dan get him ready for the fight. He's got a little cut on the left corner of his mouth, but other than that, he looks okay. Calm even.

I catch his eye as Dan slips out of the ring and give him an encouraging smile. He doesn't smile back, but his eyes soften a bit and I know he appreciates me standing in his corner. He holds out a gloved fist to me. I'm too far away to bump it, but I hold out my fist in his direction. He seems pretty confident, which is half of boxing anyway, right?

"Ladies and gentlemen," Principal Santini says into a mic to get everyone's attention, "it's finally time for the fight that you've all been waiting for! Our resident boxing champ for three years running, Red Jackson, versus newcomer challenger, Julian VanderNeen. Both young men have already defeated two different competitors and the winner of this match will go on to the regional semi-finals."

As everyone starts cheering, I scan the crowds. My parents came early when I told them Julian would be fighting before the girls got into the ring, which was nice of them. My gaze follows along the clapping, shouting audience until it lands on Adrian and Cherry who are sitting together. If it weren't for the shared connection between me and them, they would probably never have attended a school event together. It makes me feel all warm and fuzzy inside.

"Okay boys," I hear the principal say to Red and Julian, his mouth turned away from the mic. "I want a fair, clean fight. You know the rules." He picks the mic back up and says, "Let the fight begin!"

Even louder cheering erupts from the stands as Mr. Pfizer comes to the centre of the ring. He blows his whistle to signal the start of the match and quickly backs away as Red and Julian tap their gloves together. Red has a smug smirk on his face like he thinks the match is basically over. But I know that behind Julian's calm façade lies a heart of determination and strength.

I have to remind myself that there are only three rounds which last three minutes each. Nine minutes in total. That's how long Julian has to last.

Julian knows that Red never likes to throw the first punch, so he dances around, trying to force Red into making the first move. While they move, I compare them—Red is bulkier than Julian, stronger, and more experienced. But Julian is slightly taller and clearly lighter on his feet. I hope Jules realizes that and uses it to his advantage.

The boys dance around until Mr. Smith coaxes them, reminding them that someone *has* to make the first move or they will both forfeit. His words must have meant something to Red because he throws the laziest punch ever in Julian's direction. Unfortunately, Julian doesn't realize it's a fake until it's too late and Red lands a cross punch right to Julian's chin.

To his credit, Julian recovers quickly, ducks another punch and hits Red square in the face. Red barely seems affected by it, though, and I think that must shake Julian's confidence because the rest of the round is a disaster. Julian misses a majority of his punches and blocks, giving Red a huge advantage in terms of scoring. When the bell rings to signify the end of the first round, Julian drops his hands and quickly scoots out of the ring toward me and Dan.

"What are you doing, Julian?" Dan whispers fiercely. "You gave up before you even started."

"I know," he says weakly, wiping sweat off his forehead with his arm.

Jules only has a minute to recover and I don't want my uncle making him feel worse so I cut in quickly saying, "Don't do this to yourself, Jules.

You have plenty of advantages over Red. Use them."

"Like what?" he asks wearily.

"He's *so* slow," I tell him, handing him a towel to dry off his sweat. "He gets away with it because every punch is powerful."

Dan nods. "She's right. Don't let him get away with it. Blocking every one of his punches is going to tire you out too quickly, so bob and weave. You're much lighter on your feet; you should be able to evade him easily."

"Okay, but that doesn't score me points," he says.

"You'll find your opportunity," Dan says. "Now get up there."

Julian nods, but just before he goes, I grab his arm and say quietly, "He's weaker on his left side."

Julian gives me a small smile. Maybe he already knew that, but I'm glad I could reaffirm it for him. Being right-handed, he should be able to use that information to his advantage.

The second round goes much better. Even though I know Jules is tired, he makes a very conscious effort to evade Red's moves. I can tell Red is getting frustrated that Julian seems to have more energy this time around, which makes it easier for Jules to land a few clean punches himself.

Right before the end of the round, Red throws a jab that's just a little too low and it hits Julian below his belt. Julian is momentarily thrown off-guard by the illegal move and Red takes his chance at giving Julian a swift hook to the head that almost knocks him down. The crowd boos.

"Ref!" Dan yells, going straight up to the ring and looking like he wants to strangle either Mr. Pfizer or Red. "That was way below the belt! Call it."

But Mr. Pfizer already has the whistle in his mouth because he knows Red was in the wrong. The judges give Red a stern look and I know he'll be penalized for his actions. They resume with thirty seconds on the clock, during which Julian lands two more clean hits.

Jules is breathing pretty hard when he comes back down to us. I help him take a drink of water so he doesn't have to take his gloves off while Dan praises him for doing so much better this round.

"He's tired," Dan says happily.

"Well, so am I," Julian huffs. "I don't know how to get through this round."

"Three more minutes," Dan says, patting him on the shoulder. "That's all it is. Just do what you did this round. Except with more uppercuts. Your uppercuts are amazing and you haven't used a single one this match."

"I haven't had a chance," Jules complains. "He must be really afraid of them because he's always got a glove close to his chin."

"The slip," I say.

Jules gives me a look. "I'm not very good at it, you know that."

"So?" I say. "He's slow. You need to do it. Slip, fake, uppercut. You can do it."

Julian looks at Dan who simply nods with a thoughtful frown. It's time for Julian to get back in the ring, and now I seriously regret having chewed down all my fingernails before the fight even started.

Both boys are tired and it's showing. Still, Julian has the advantage of being naturally quicker than Red and he's definitely using it now that he knows Red can't quite keep up. Neither one of them lands a good hit for at least the first minute.

Julian lands a couple of punches, which clearly annoys Red to the point that he actually wraps his arms around Julian's upper body to stop him. I give Dan a bewildered look but he's miles ahead of me.

"Hey!!" Dan shouts, his face red, veins popping out of his forehead. "Get your hands off him!"

Dan looks ready to wring Red's neck but Mr. Pfizer quickly and effectively breaks the two boys up. There's a momentary pause, during which Dan goes over to Red's coach to exchange angry words with him. I look up at Julian and he looks confused, even though he's trying to hide it.

When Dan comes back, I say to him, "What was that all about?"

He keeps his eyes on Julian as Mr. Pfizer signals for them to resume their fight. Then he says to me, "Red was clinching, which you're not supposed to do in an amateur high school boxing match. You basically just hug your opponent until they stop hitting you."

"Oh," I say. "I guess Julian wasn't prepared for that."

"There's no reason he should have been," Dan spits out. "Red and his coach should know better." He looks at me and gives me a reassuring pat on the shoulder. "Don't worry; points will be deducted from Red for his belligerence."

I nod. I wish I'd been paying closer attention to who was landing which hits so I could have a better idea of who was ahead. I don't know, but I do know that Julian is doing very well and that Red has already made two illegal moves.

With just one minute left, Julian finds his magical moment when Red moves in for a left hook. Julian, knowing that Red's left side is weaker, ducks just in time for Red to miss. Then while Red is still following through on his punch, Julian leans into what should have been a jab to Red's chest. But when Red goes to block him, Julian quickly changes his tactic to land the hardest uppercut I've ever seen him throw.

Red's head snaps back and he's just off-balance enough that he actually stumbles backwards, straight onto the ground. The crowd goes wild as Mr. Pfizer begins his count.

I'm stunned but Julian's victory is short-lived as Red recovers around the three-second mark. Still, it's amazing that Julian was able to knock Red to the ground when Red hasn't done that to Julian yet. I'm sure it'll score him huge points.

Thirty seconds left and they are both giving it all they've got. When the bell goes off, they are both very reluctant to stop. In fact, Mr. Pfizer has to get between them and forcefully tell them that the match is over. But Red is staring at Julian like he'd like to beat his brains out and Julian looks like he'd like to still be standing over a knocked out Red.

They finally retreat to their corners after threatening each other using only their eyes and we all wait impatiently for the scores to be announced. I tell Julian how amazing he was, and how I can't believe he knocked Red down and all that. But I stop when I hear someone start to chant "Ju-li-an! Ju-li-an!"

Others start joining into the chant and Julian has the decency to look humble and proud at the same time. The three judges, with their heads bent towards each other, keep looking around the gym. They look like they're arguing with each other and a moment later, I find out why.

The head judge comes up to the centre of the ring with a mic in hand. He waits while the chanting dies down and then says, "This year's boxing champion is...Red Jackson."

He doesn't sound enthusiastic and at first there is no sound except for a few gasps as Red scoots back into the ring with a smug grin on his face. The grin quickly disappears when people start to shift uncomfortably, and a few others give some polite applause. Red takes his belt, looking angry that no one cares that he won.

Then someone—who sounds very much like Cherry—shouts, "Julian for people's choice!"

The judge clears his throat. "There's no...people's choice. This is a high school competition."

"Peo-ple's choice!" And the chanting starts all over again.

Julian ducks his head, but I can see the smile spreading across his face. I slap Julian's back with a laugh and he laughs too because what else is there to do?

The judge sighs and then motions to Red. "Your champion everyone." Again, he says it with all the enthusiasm of announcing that he's getting a root canal.

Red rolls his eyes as everyone continues chanting "People's choice!" Then he surprises everyone by motioning Julian into the ring with him. Julian looks stunned but he climbs through the ropes, inciting even louder cheering. I almost think Red is up to something, but then he begrudgingly holds out a hand which Julian shakes.

Red shakes his head and leaves the ring. Julian takes one look around, raises his fists in a victory that he hasn't technically won, and is ushered out of the ring by Mr. Pfizer.

"Julian, you are too cool," I say to him.

Jules laughs and then closes his eyes, looking like he could fall asleep standing on the spot.

Dan says to me, "Hey, you need to get back to the locker room. You still have your own match coming up, you know."

Crap. I still have to fight

CHAPTER TWENTY-THREE

When they set up the matches, I'd been hoping that maybe they'd set me up with Emily or even Marissa, because I think they would have been a little easy on me. But no—they set me up with Denny. As nice as she can be sometimes, she's a fierce competitor. And now that I'm seeing her on game day, I know she's going to take me down the first chance she gets.

Denny always makes the first move, so as soon as the bell rings I get my arms up in a defensive position. I know it makes me sound like a wimp, but I'm more afraid of her hurting me than losing this match. As I predicted, Denny takes the first swing, but she only hits my glove, since I haven't moved them out of my face yet.

She tries a couple more times to goad me into doing something other than just waiting for her. I try once to knock a good right cross to her head, but she ducks easily and hits me in the side where I left a wide-open gap.

"Come on, Elli!" Dan yells from my corner. "You're better than that. Get moving!"

I can feel my face heat up from the embarrassment of being called out by my coach. But I don't want to let him down, so I channel my inner Julian and get my butt in gear. I start to do a little better, even getting a few good hits and blocks in.

I don't have much of an advantage over Denny, but the first two rounds fly by without much incident. I think I might even be able to win until we get to the third round. I try to remind myself that it's only three minutes, but I'm so tired now. On top of that, I think Denny just realized that I'm better than she originally thought because she has suddenly stepped up her game.

I try to keep up but there's no way I could have seen the uppercut coming. I feel myself fall backwards, I hear my uncle's disembodied voice telling me to get up, I hear Mr. Pfizer counting, but I can't move. I'm stunned and my neck hurts and there's no way. As soon as he gets to ten, Denny kneels down next to me, yanking off her helmet.

"Elli!" she shouts in my face. "I'm so sorry, are you okay?"

It takes me a minute to focus on her face, and then I say, "You knocked me out."

She nods a lot while Dan and my cutman—the guy who looks after bruises, swelling, and cuts during the matches—rush into the ring. "I know. I'm so sorry. I've never done that before."

I start laughing as the cutman removes my helmet and examines my face. Denny gives me a look like I'm crazy so I explain, "You deserved to win that. Don't worry, I'm not hurt."

Denny still looks unsure, so I push away the cutman's hands and get up on my own. I only sway a little, but then I offer Denny my hand and she shakes it with a huge grin as people cheer for her victory.

*　　　*　　　*

That night, my parents take me and Dan out for dinner. It's a little awkward, but not as bad as I thought it would be. They're trying to get along—whether for my sake or their own, it doesn't really matter. I'm just glad to have my family together for at least one night, celebrating how much of a champ I was for taking that knockout so coolly.

That's literally what my dad has been telling anyone who will listen. How cool I was when I got knocked out. It would probably make me laugh if only I hadn't be left with a black eye. Oh well.

At least I have a good excuse for skipping out on the dance tonight. Yeah, you read that right. I've been planning on not going for about a week now. I know—I had a really awesome group of friends to go with and a great date, but this is a bigger picture kind of thing. See I told Julian and Cherry to meet me there…

Which, of course, they won't. Because I won't be there. But they will be. And maybe they'll get over whatever happened in the past and even start being friends again.

I tell my parents that I kind of don't feel well as a precursor to me later on telling them that I might not go to the dance. They're only half paying attention—although my mom did mention that I had that beautiful dress—because they're being all…flirty with each other? I don't know, it's kind of weird. Anyway, I tell my mom I can wear the dress to the next school dance.

She kind of nods and then whispers something in my dad's ear. He blushes (I've never seen that happen) and then kind of chuckles. I exchange a what-is-going-on look with my uncle who asks me very pointedly if I would like him to take me home since I'm not feeling well. I agree and we hastily exit without my parents taking much notice.

"Ugh, thank you for saving me from that," Dan says as soon as we're both in his clunker of a car.

I laugh. "I don't remember the last time I saw them like that."

Dan is quiet for a few minutes and then he says to me, "I'm really proud of you, Elli."

"Thanks," I say softly. I'm sure he's saying it just to be nice.

"No, I mean it," he says as if he's reading my mind. Or maybe I spoke out loud again. "Not like your dad. He's obligated to feel proud of you. But me—I got to teach you, I got to coach you. And you were amazing! And on top of that, you were great with Julian. I really don't think he could have done so well without you there."

"Thank you, Uncle Dan," I say. I don't know how to say how much his words mean to me. It's like I also feel proud of me, and Julian, and Dan, and it's just too much emotion for one sentence. Instead, I ask, "How are things going…like with Liz and stuff?"

I'm sure Dan can see right through my thinly veiled question. He doesn't say anything as he parks the car at my house. Then he turns to me and says, "I'm an alcoholic, Elli. But I'm trying."

"Good," I say. "I'm glad. I'm sorry that I…" Caught him being an alcoholic? I can't even finish the sentence.

"No, *I'm* sorry," he says. He pats my cheek, glances at my black eye, and adds, "You can still go to the dance if you want. It's not that bad."

"Oh that!" I laugh, touching my sore eye. "No, it's not that. I'm kind of proud of it, actually. But really…I can't go tonight. It's complicated, but it's for the best. Trust me."

Dan just shakes his head with a wry smile. I go inside and exhale with relief. The fight is over and I never have to box again if I don't want to. My friends are going to find each other at the dance tonight. My parents are happy, at least for right now. Dan is…well, still Dan, but less pickled.

I do feel badly for Adrian though. I decide to text him to let him know that I won't be at the dance. I didn't get much of a chance to talk to him after the fight and I hope he'll understand. I'm a little disappointed that he never texts me back, but maybe he's too busy preparing for the dance that he doesn't even know I texted him. Oh well, I'll have to deal with it later.

I'm having a wonderful nap in the bath when I wake up to loud banging. It's my dad, saying something about a boy or something. I'm half asleep—and freezing, I might add. How long was I asleep?

"What did you say, Dad?" I ask after putting on a robe and opening the door.

"There's a boy at the door for you," he says, a mischievous look in his eyes.

"A boy! What boy?" I say, dreading that Julian has come to give me a piece of his mind for ditching him at the dance with Cherry.

"Well, it's not Julian," Dad drawls with amusement. Good grief, what are he and my mother up to lately? Nevermind. I do not want to know the answer to that question.

"Okay..." I say slowly. I go to my room and quickly throw on sweat pants and a t-shirt, a decision I immediately regret when I go downstairs and see Adrian all dressed up in a suit.

He smiles at me. My insides turn to mush.

"Adrian," I say dumbly. "You're not at the dance."

His smile grows. "And neither are you. What's up?"

I look down at my ramshackle appearance and heat rushes to my face. "I told you that I wasn't—"

"Feeling well. Uh huh," he says like he totally does not believe it at all. "I know what you're up to."

"You do?" I ask. "And what is that?"

He looks me up and down, giving me a look that says he still thinks I'm pretty in this get-up and says, "Tell you what—since I'm already dressed up, why don't you go out with me tonight?" He sees me hesitate and adds, "Or do you not want to know what you missed at the dance?"

Okay, he's got me there. And judging by the smug look on his face, he knows it, too. I'm about to go find my parents to tell them I'm going out after all when I discover them lurking around the corner, listening to every word.

"Umm… Mom, Dad, this is Adrian," I say, pointing to my very well-dressed almost-boyfriend.

"Nice to meet you," Adrian says confidently, extending his hand out to my dad and then my mom. He's so proper.

"Well, Elli, you're not going out like that, are you?" Mom says meaningfully.

"Give me two minutes," I say to Adrian.

I rush upstairs, shimmy into the coral blue dress, throw my hair up in a way that says, "I care, but not that much," and then apply make-up as carefully and quickly as I can. It's been five minutes, but I'm sure Adrian didn't take that literally.

Right?

I come back down and Adrian gives me another once-over, this one clearly indicating that he thinks I'm very pretty. At least, I hope that's what it means.

Then he stares at my beautiful, brand-new heels and says, "Comfier shoes."

I don't even ask—I just find a pair of flats that don't look horrible with the dress, and then we're out the door.

"Nice dress," Adrian says as he starts leading me down the street, my hand tucked into the crook of his arm.

"Thanks," I say sweetly.

"Goes well with the shiner."

"Shut up."

"Really, you look beautiful, Elli."

I blush, and say, "You don't look too bad yourself."

We walk for a few minutes and then I ask, "Are you going to tell me what I missed at the dance?"

"Let's see... Oh! Chad and Heather were totally making out in the corner. It was gross."

He's teasing me, but I can't help laughing. "Come on. Were Julian and Cherry there?"

Adrian nods. "I hung out with them for a few minutes while we waited for you. I didn't tell them you were never going to show up. They've probably figured it out by now, though."

"Oh," I say. I don't know what I expected him to tell me. It doesn't sound like he was at the dance long enough to see anything else.

"But they were dancing together when I left," he announces.

"REALLY?!" I squeak.

Adrian's eyes grow huge as he sticks a finger in his ear. "I think you shattered my ear drum."

"Sorry," I say, but I can't help how excited I still sound.

"What?" he jokingly shouts.

I swat at his arm. "Where are we going?"

"We're almost there," he says, like that's in any way an answer to my question.

Turns out we're going to this adorable little ice cream bar. Adrian tells me that normally it would be crowded with kids, but since there's the dance at school tonight, it's not so busy. We even manage to snag a corner booth.

"You're so different than I first thought you'd be," I say. I know I've caught him off-guard by the look he gives me.

"How did you think I'd be?" he says.

Now I feel weird. I don't know how to be polite about saying that I thought he was a dumb jock. "I guess I got some misinformation about you. Like...that you were this big flirt, and how everyone's just in love with you because you're a good hockey player or whatever."

Adrian lifts an eyebrow and half-smiles at me. "And now?" he asks, sounding very sweetly shy.

"I think you're very...sweet. Perceptive. Optimistic," I say. He smiles at that, and I wonder if anyone has ever complimented him that way before.

"Thanks." He stares at his half-melted ice cream for a few seconds and then says, "To tell you the truth, Elli, I am kind of shallow. Or at least, I used to be. Then I met you, and you were this cool girl who stood up to literally the biggest, meanest guy in our school for the most—how to say this nicely?—uncool guy in school and I guess it inspired me. I think you inspired a lot of people."

"Aw Adrian—"

"Plus, you know, you're hot. So that helps."

He gives me a teasing smile, but I know he means it, too, and it makes me blush. I quickly scoop some ice cream into my mouth to cool my face off.

"I guess you're exactly what I thought you were," I tease back, smiling to let him know I don't mean it.

"Yup, you've got me all figured out," he says sarcastically.

"Tell me something about you that no one else knows," I say.

He purses his lips like he's not sure he wants to answer. Then he looks up at me with serious eyes and says, "My grandma died last year and I cried myself to sleep for two weeks straight."

My eyes widen. I almost want to ask if he's serious, but I can tell by his eyes that he is. "I'm so sorry," I say softly. "I guess you were close?"

He swallows hard and nods. "Your turn."

I respect that he wants to move on from this topic, so I go for something lighter. "My birthday is next week. And yeah, there are people who know that. But none of my new friends here do. You're the first."

Adrian smiles. "Well, well, well. We'll have to find something fun to do."

Adrian and I stay at the ice cream bar for a good two hours before we decide to call it a night. He holds my hand as he walks me home, and the warm strength of his grasp makes me feel almost like I could stay here in Canada and not miss Hawaii so much anymore. It's like I can finally stop feeling like I'm betraying my home if I actually like it here.

And when we kiss goodnight, I think I even forget what the ocean sounds like for a minute.

CHAPTER TWENTY-FOUR

Things are so different today. Or maybe it's just that I feel different. I mean, if you'd told me five months ago that I'd compete in a boxing championship alongside a nerd-turned-athlete, hang out with an edgy girl, and date the cutest guy at school I never would have believed you. If you'd told me that I would eventually stop missing the ocean, the sights and smells of Hawaii, and the island breeze in favour of man-made parks, skating rinks, and crazy temperature changes, I probably would have had you admitted to a psychiatric hospital.

Anyway, people are giving me a lot of attention today. Even Red, when I walked past him in the hallway this morning, gave me a headnod in greeting. I returned it, even though it felt totally weird. I don't know whether people are acknowledging me because of the black eye, or because they thought I was really good at the tourney; or maybe it's just because they know I'm friends with Julian. Either way, it kind of feels good.

An even better feeling is when I get to lunch and Cherry is sitting in my spot next to Julian. I watch them for a moment, thrilled to see them interacting in a shy-because-I-like-you kind of way. It's cute.

I sit down across from them and say hi like there's nothing weird going on.

"Uh," Julian looks at a non-existent watch on his forearm, "you're two days late for the dance, Elli."

"Whoops," I say, pulling a textbook out of my backpack just to see if that annoys him as much as when he does that to me.

"Whoops?" He says, putting a hand on top of the book to prevent me from opening it.

Gotcha.

"Didn't you get my message?" I say, hoping to pin some of the blame on Adrian for not telling them.

"Oh hey!" I hear a voice behind me. It's Adrian. He sits next to me. "Look, you guys, I found her."

Julian rolls his eyes and Cherry, who hasn't said anything yet, looks between us and I know I'm caught. Then she smiles at me while Julian's not watching and I smile back.

"Did you guys have a good time?" I ask.

"Yes, we did," Cherry answers emphatically.

Julian looks at me, and I think I see gratitude in his eyes. Then they crinkle up a bit and he says, "Nice shiner."

I laugh. Julian has three cuts on his face, one of which has a couple of stitches in it. His chin is bruised, and it looks like he hasn't shaved since before the tournament. I could look a lot worse, is what I'm saying.

"Soo...I kind of have an announcement," Julian says suddenly. The three of us look at him expectantly. "I'm supposed to go to the boxing regionals."

"But you came in second," Adrian states the obvious.

Julian nods. "Yeah...but apparently some other guy got caught cheating and was forced to pull out and Mr. Santini recommended me as a replacement. Soo..." he shrugs.

"Jules! That's awesome," I say, though I can tell he's not sure about this news. "Are you going to do it?"

He shrugs again. "I dunno. Maybe. I have a few days to think about it."

Julian could be going to regionals and he's being nonchalant about it! I can't even understand that. But I know Julian—I know he likes to think through his decisions thoroughly—so I don't push it.

*   *   *

Today is my birthday. I'm a little sad to be honest. My friends back home all sent me little emails and messages, and I even got a few cards in the mail. But that just made me sadder. I mean, don't get me wrong—I love my new friends and my new life here. I've grown accustomed to this beautiful place where I'm now living. But I always had the most fantastic beach parties on my birthday. It was like a special thing that can never be repeated again.

But Julian, Cherry, and Adrian are intent on giving me the best first Canadian birthday ever. So far I've eaten pretty much every maple-flavoured treat ever made, including fudge, candies, snow cones, pancakes with real syrup (not that fake store-brand stuff), maple bacon, and maple taffy.

Now I'm being led, blindfolded, to who-knows-where so that I can have more of an adventure. Yay. If only they'd take the blindfold off…

"Just a few more minutes, Elli," Adrian says, squeezing my hand. Comforting.

We're on a bus, didn't I mention that? Have you ever been blindfolded on a bus before? Not an easy thing to accomplish. Anyway, the bus finally stops and we get off, and Adrian's still holding my hand which would be so nice if only I could see.

"Can I take this thing off yet?" I ask, fingering the scarf covering my eyes.

"Almost," Cherry says, laughing a bit.

Ugh. Because I'm wearing flip flops, I can feel that we're walking over grass. Did we come to some sort of park? Maybe. Then I feel something more familiar. The ground becomes uneven and hot, and I feel the unmistakable sting of tiny grains of sand squishing up into my toes.

"Where *are* we?" I ask in bewilderment.

Finally, one of them takes off the blindfold. We're on a beach and there's a huge expanse of water in front of us. I know it's not the ocean—it doesn't smell like the ocean, and the waves aren't very big. But some people are splashing around and others sunbathing. Off in the distance I see a few boats on the water.

Julian laughs as he takes in the look on my face. "It's just Lake Ontario," he explains. "But we thought maybe it would make you feel a little closer to home."

"That's...a *huge* lake," I say. What I really want to say is, "That's the sweetest thing anyone's ever done for me," but I've cried where there is sand before and it never ends well.

"Yup," Adrian says. "There's no surfing, but we managed to scrounge up a sailboat for you."

"Really?" I squeak. "I love sailing." I know I sound wistful and probably a little pathetic, but they just look so proud of themselves for thinking of it.

So then we're on a sailboat with our picnic lunch in front of us. We're working on our first tans of the season (though it took a little work to convince Jules that the computer screen look was just not working for him).

We've pretty much eaten everything in the cooler, so I'm surprised when Adrian reaches in and says, "Huh, there's something else in here."

"Ughhh," I say, holding my stomach. I'm laying down with my eyes closed, halfway to a food coma. "I don't think I could eat anything else."

"Nah, you'll like this," he says and something about his tone of voice makes me sit up.

"What is it?" I ask, curious now.

Adrian looks at Cherry and Julian who have matching ridiculous grins on their faces, and now I'm really curious because something is definitely going on and I have to know what it is.

Adrian pulls out an envelope and hands it to me. I really wasn't expecting another gift, but I open the envelope anyway and inside IS A ROUND TRIP TICKET TO HAWAII AND I CAN'T EVEN.

"Wait, what?" I say, dumbstruck. "Is this for real?"

"Yup," Adrian says, rubbing my shoulder and kind of shaking me because I guess I'm not moving at all.

"We asked your parents," Julian says. "They were okay with it. They even pitched in a little."

"They had one stipulation," Cherry adds.

There's a special glint in her eyes when I sigh and ask, "Which was?"

"They didn't want you to go alone," she says. And then before I can protest, she quickly says, "So I'm going with you!"

"*Really?*" I'm sure my voice is so high-pitched right now that only dogs can hear it, but she manages to answer anyway.

"Yes!" She's really excited now and I wonder how long they've had to keep this a secret from me. "We're going for two weeks, and staying with friends, and I want you to show me everything!"

"Oh, you guys!" I hug Cherry, and Julian, and I kiss Adrian, and then I try to hug them all at once, but I can't, but I try anyway. This is the *best* birthday present ever. I don't even know how to tell them. "I don't know what to say!"

"Say you'll bring me a souvenir," Julian helpfully tells me.

"Say you'll bring me next time." Adrian winks. *I wish.*

*   *   *

School has ended and Cherry and I are preparing for our trip. I've already made extensive plans so that she can experience as much as possible and I can still spend a fair amount of time visiting with my friends. I think it'll be fun playing tourist in Hawaii. I never thought I'd be doing that, but then I never thought anything that's happened in the last six months would have happened.

My uncle seems to be doing really well. I don't see him very often, but I know he's working, staying sober, and also training Julian. Yeah, Julian decided to do regionals after all. They're not until the end of summer, so he'll have time to get a lot of practice in, but I think it'll be good for him to not have to focus on school. He might even win. Who knows?

My mom moved back home. She and my dad haven't been fighting at all, which is a relief, but also a little weird. Weird in a good way, of course. I much prefer it this way. But I wonder if they've saved their relationship at the cost of my dad's relationship with his brother. I mean, I know it's not my business, but I wonder if Dan staying away is something that is helping them be closer together. In any case, I think they'll figure it out. I'm just glad to have my family back in one piece.

As I pack for my trip, I briefly wonder if it'll be weird seeing Kai again, but I've moved on from that and I can only assume he has, too. I look forward to seeing my friends again. I wonder if any of them have changed like I feel I have.

Not gonna lie though—I don't miss old Elli. New Elli is a lot cooler than old Elli. And I like it that way.

Did you think the story was over?

Because it's not…

Read on for a sneak peek at the sequel:

STANDUP GUY

CHAPTER ONE

Elli

Picture yourself on a cruise ship that you'd always wanted to go on but never have because everyone always told you that it was for tourists and it was basically a big waste of money. Now picture being that tourist because you are no longer a Hawaiian—you are now Canadian and you've brought a Canadian friend with you to Hawaii.

Of course, we're not talking about you. We're talking about me and Cherry. Cherry and I have spent the last two weeks in Hawaii, meeting my friends, seeing my favourite spots, and playing tourist in places I've never even been to. We're ending our trip with a four-hour snorkeling cruise, just the two of us.

It was amazing seeing my friends and getting to enjoy the Hawaiian climate again, but I have to say...I really miss my new home in Canada. Call me crazy but I'm happy with my new life. Weird, I know. But there's a lot waiting for me back home. New friends, snow, boxing...

Adrian.

"Elli!" Cherry grabs my hand and tugs me all the way to the other side of the boat. "Look, look, look!"

I smile down at the part of the water she's pointing to. It's so clear that you can see all kinds of multicoloured fish and coral. The boat is slowing down near a crescent-shaped little island called Molokini. This is where we'll be able to get out in the water and see all the cute little fish that Cherry's so excited about.

Once the boat has stopped, the captain and his first mates give us the basics of snorkeling (which I've done before but Cherry hasn't) and the rules, one of which includes no swimming up to the island. I can tell that disappoints Cherry, but the iconic little crater island is a marine and bird life preservation area so no one is ever allowed up there. She'll still have fun looking around in the water, though.

Cherry rips off her sundress and flings it on a random seat before grabbing some snorkeling gear from one of the first mates. While she's getting the goggles on her head, she's totally unaware that the guy is checking her out. Admittedly, she has a very nice figure and she looks older than she is.

She looks back at me and gives me a goofy grin around the mouthpiece. "Less jump in togeder!" she tries to shout at me.

I laugh as I put my own goggles and snorkel on. Then I take her hand and we run and jump off the edge of the boat together. We crash into the warm water and I shut my eyes, momentarily forgetting that there's no real need. I come back up and search around for Cherry but she must have dived further under. I wait for what feels like forever, so long that I think maybe she's drowning. But then she pops up a few feet away from me.

She spits her mouthpiece out and says, "Elli! That was amazing. You should have gone as far as I did. There's all kinds of cool stuff down here. Come look!"

Just as quickly as she came up, she's gone again, but at least this time she leaves her snorkel out of the water so she can breathe. I put my head down and as soon as I do, she takes my hand. With her free hand, she starts pointing out all kinds of fish, some that look so close she could grab them, which of course, she tries to do. She never succeeds but it's fun to watch her try.

Oh! She's making a little camera motion at me. I spring to the surface so I can go up and get the underwater camera we rented. Oh, Julian's going to love seeing these pictures, I just know it. I bet he'd even be able to identify the fish and coral we're seeing. And if not, he'd look it up. He's a big nerd. But he's also my other best friend, so I really mean that in an affectionate kind of way.

He's also Cherry's boyfriend now. Thanks to me. Yup. I did it. I got them together, which was nothing short of a miracle, let me tell you. Anyway, that's another story for another day. Cherry's waving at me from the water so I jump back in with the camera. We pass the camera back and forth, taking ridiculous photos of each other snorkeling and posing like swimsuit models—she certainly fits the part better—and of all the fancy fish and coral.

The snorkeling trip is the last touristy thing we do before we go home. My friends all come to the airport to say goodbye to us. My former crush, Kai is there too and I give him a hug. To be honest, I thought when I first saw him again that I'd get that crazy feeling in my stomach all over again. But then, surprisingly, I didn't. It was just like seeing any other guy.

Cherry seems a little sad to be leaving and I totally get why. My friends were so accepting of her, they just folded her into the group like it was no big deal. And to be honest...there's no place on Earth that's like Hawaii. I think—I hope that now she gets why I was kind of a space case when she first met me, and why I was terrified of the ice the first time she took me skating.

I let Cherry take the window seat on the way back because I got to have it on the way there. When we're up in the air, she waves and says, "Goodbye, Hawaii. I'll always love you."

"Wow," I say with a little giggle. "I think you may be even more in love with Hawaii than I am."

"Seriously, though," she says putting her hand flat on the window, "that was a blast. Thank you so much for taking me."

I snort. "You bought yourself a ticket," I jokingly remind her.

She turns to me with a wry grin. "Yeah, I know. But you could have given it to someone else."

I briefly think about who that other person would have been. Adrian, so I could have shown off my cute boyfriend to my friends (like Lily, who totally stole Kai after I moved, BTW)? Or Julian, since he's been like my BFF since the first day I started at my new school, who's totally rocking the rookie boxing world right now?

I give her a look. Obviously neither of those options would have happened. "Like I would have ever."

She bursts out laughing. "Well, I gotta say, I'm happy you're on the return flight."

I laugh. "I guess I'm a little more in love with Canada than I first thought I'd be."

Never in the first sixteen years of my life did I ever think I would say those words. I'm seventeen now, though.

Julian

"Left! Left side! Get on your left! Defense! What are you doing?"

These words race through my head as if they were my own, but they're not. I'm being yelled at by my coach, Dan, who also happens to be my best friend's uncle. How did I, the nerdiest kid in school, become this boxing guy? Well, it's her fault—Ella's. I'm not still mad about it, but—

"Duck!"

I duck almost before Dan shouts the word at me and my opponent's glove misses my head by a fraction of an inch. Unfortunately, he manages to get in three more hits before I can fully recover. If Ella were here, she'd probably knock me up the side of my head for letting him score that many points on me. But she's not here. She's in Hawaii. With my girlfriend.

"Get your head in the game, Jules!" Dan shouts. I don't need to look at him to know that he's giving me an angry scowl.

There are thirty seconds left on the clock. I don't know if other boxers keep track of the time like I do, but I find it helps me focus if I count while I'm boxing. Dan would probably tell me I'm thinking too much and to spend all my energy on fighting, but I can't help it.

Fifteen...

Fourteen...

Thirteen...

Twelve...

Eleven...

At ten, I hear the audience start to count down and I focus on getting in as many last shots as I can. When the bell goes, I have to consciously not sigh in relief. My opponent wasn't tough, but he's quick and he kept me moving the entire time. It was exhausting, so I'm glad it's over.

We take our gloves off and shake hands. His hand is sweaty and I am repulsed until I realize my hand is just as sweaty as, if not more so, than his. Oh well. This is just a part of my newfound hobby, I guess. Suddenly, I hear my name being announced.

"Julian VanderNeen, winner of this tournament," the voice says.

My mouth gapes open. I can't believe it. The closest I've come to winning anything this summer was getting third place in a tournament a few weeks ago. Dan puts his hands on my shoulders and shakes me, grinning like crazy and I can't help smiling back.

I, Julian VanderNeen, biggest nerd in my entire school, have won a boxing tournament. Take that, meatheads.

Someone slaps me hard on the back and by the strength of it I know exactly who it is. I turn around and there's Red Jackson, my former bully and boxer extraordinaire, grimacing at me. No wait, he's actually smiling. He sticks out his hand and I slap his palm-to-palm and then back-to-back and then we knock elbows. Why? Because even though we shouldn't be friends, we still developed our own handshake over the summer while we trained at the same gym.

To be clear, we weren't "training together." But Dan happened to land himself a good job at the same gym that just happened to be the one Red and his coach use. And Red just happened to give me some tips and I just happen to be helping him with his summer school final project.

"Hey, man," he says. It's weird hearing him call me man, instead of him just shoving me in a locker as soon as he sees me like he used to do. "That was a hard finish. Good job."

Again, I have a really hard time with this tenuous relationship we have based on me having almost beat him at our school's boxing tourney. Before then, Red used to push me around pretty much every chance he got until Ella stood up to him one day and roped me into the ring.

Ha, I am a nerd.

"Yeah, I doubt I would have won if you were in this tournament," I tell him. Though I said it because I prefer to be on his good side, it's actually the truth, too. Red is a stellar boxer.

He scowls. "You know I'm not allowed to compete until summer school's over. It sucks," he spits out.

I nod. Red's parents weren't very happy about his near-failing grades at the end of the school year and they forbade him from boxing unless he does well in summer school. Which is how we ended up helping each other out. It's still weird, though.

"Julian, I am *so* proud of you," Dan says, as he helps me unwrap my hands and gives me a water bottle. "And I know if Elli were here, she would be, too."

I smile and then take a giant gulp of water. "I'm sure she would be."

I say goodbye to Red and look around to see if either of my parents eventually showed up for my tournament today. I know Mom doesn't really like boxing—she thinks it's too violent—but Dad was really impressed with how much weight I lost from training. But now that I see that he's not here, I guess he doesn't actually care that much about how good I am at boxing.

"They didn't come," Dan says quietly, giving me a pitying look.

I stifle a sigh. I had promised myself no more sighing, at least not in front of other people. Whenever I do, it practically begs others to ask what's wrong and sometimes there isn't something wrong. Sometimes you're just disappointed and you just feel like sighing. But I don't do that anymore.

"It's alright," I say in a flat voice, looking down at my shoes. "They were probably busy."

"Well, if you were my son, I'd never want to miss a single match," Dan says.

I look up at him. Dan's a pretty hard coach, but he's also a soft-hearted friend and his words mean a lot to me. I smile because I know he's trying to make me feel better, and the effort itself does make me feel better.

"Let me take you out," he says. "You deserve a cheeseburger."

"Oh, a cheeseburger!" I say with mock enthusiasm. In truth, I haven't been allowed a cheeseburger or anything remotely like it in months. "How fancy."

"Unless you want something else," Dan says, taking my sarcasm seriously.

I cling to the chance of having something that's actually tasty. "No, no. Burgers are fine."

I go to the change rooms to get dressed and gather all of my things. The guy I just beat is in there, pulling a sweatshirt over his head.

"Good match," I tell him. He just grunts. Meh. You win some, you lose some.

Dan takes me to Five Guys, this awesome place that serves humongous burgers with massive sides of fries to match, and tells me to get whatever I want. I don't need to be told twice. Opportunities like this don't come along too often for me anymore.

While I eat, Dan says to me, "I'm really proud of you Julian. I can't believe how far you've come."

I smile a little and shrug because I don't know if it's appropriate to say that I'm also proud of him and how far he's come. When I first met him, he was homeless, unemployed, and struggling to overcome his alcoholism. Today, he is none of those things.

"Let me ask you something, though," he continues. "Why do you keep boxing when it's obviously not your favourite thing to do?"

"I like it," I say. I mean it, too. I like it more than I thought I would.

"Is that really it?" he probes. I hate probing questions.

"Well..." I scratch my head. "I guess I like being good at something that people actually notice," I admit.

"Oh." He seems surprised. "So...it's not about Elli."

This time, I do sigh. We have this conversation twice a week and twice a week I have to remind Dan that there is nothing, absolutely *nothing* romantic going on between me and Ella. We are *friends*. We *do not* like each other like that.

"Dan..."

He puts his hands up in surrender and chuckles. "Okay, I'm sorry."

I shake my head and go back to digging into my burger because it tastes like freedom and my former life of not being semi-athletic.

MORE FROM THE KNOCKOUT GIRL SERIES!

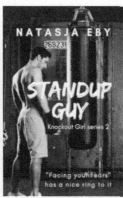

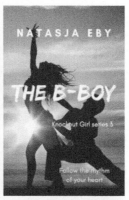

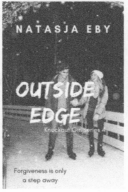

A NOTE FROM THE AUTHOR

Thank you so much for reading *Knockout Girl!* I loved telling this story of a girl who finds herself through friendship and boxing. But most importantly, I loved showing what can happen when one person stands up to bullying. Sometimes all it takes is one drop to start a wave.

If you loved the book (or even if you hated it), would you consider leaving a review? It takes a lot of time, effort, and tears to put an entire book together from scratch. Reviews help authors know what they did right and wrong, and they also help steer other readers in the right direction.

Don't forget—the story isn't over. There's still more to tell and more to explore about these loveable—and sometimes not-so-loveable—characters. Thank for coming on this ride with me, it's been a blast!

—Natasja ♥

ABOUT THE AUTHOR

Natasja is a librarian and the self-published author of *My Best Friend's Brother/The Summer I Turned Into a Girl* (Createspace 2012), a 2011 National Novel Writing Month winner, *Knockout Girl* (2018), *Standup Guy* (2019), *The B-Boy* (2019), and *Rinkside* (2019). She is an avid fan and participant of NaNoWriMo and has completed several novels over the past few Novembers.

In 2019, Natasja received two Indie Originals Awards for *Knockout Girl*, one for Best Young Adult Novel and the other for Best New Author.

When she's not working on her many unfinished novels, she can be found playing video games with her husband and two kids, singing, or curled up with a good book.

Natasja lives just outside of Toronto—close enough for good shopping and far enough to avoid the traffic.

Follow her on social media:
Facebook!
Twitter! @natasjaeby
Instagram! @natasjaeby
YouTube!
Goodreads!

Made in the USA
Monee, IL
18 October 2020